A Beggar's Tune

Written by Jeffery Jay Luhn

Vers.10/06/2021

1

A Beggar's Tune

Other books by Jeffery Jay Luhn

"The Altered Gene" 2019
"The Church of Minor Adjustments. Book One" 2020

This book is dedicated to my loving wife Lauren.
My partner in all things good.

A special thanks go out to several musicians that inspired this tale,
especially Johnny Fabulous and a xylophone player named Riz, whose
last name I never learned.

Chapter One

Kelly pushed his sleeping bag down to free his arms. The cold air felt good. He'd left a window open and the sound of crashing waves accompanied the pungent aroma of seaweed and salt. Kelly sensed a storm heading inland.

His camper was parked behind some trees on a dirt path at the rear of an artichoke field. The spot sat on the headlands overlooking the Monterey Bay and beyond. Once in a while a tractor would drive by during harvest season, but it was winter now and he was alone and safe. This was an especially good place because the police couldn't see his camper from the highway.

Getting rousted for illegal camping was unpleasant, and it had become more common in the last few years. Kelly had lots of locations like this along the Great Pacific Highway and he always left them spotless, even taking the time to pick up trash from other drifters.

He rubbed the stubble on his face, pulled on a pair of sweat pants, and grabbed the last clean hoody from the drawer. Kelly had a gig tonight at the Bluebird cafe in Monterey, but first he had to sneak into the showers at the community college, do laundry, and change his guitar strings.

After a cup of exceptionally strong coffee, which he finished by swirling the grits around and downing it in one big gulp, he carefully placed Anna's framed photo into a drawer.

4

The photo was Kelly's most valuable possession. Her half smile reminded him of how she would look at him before holding his head in her hands and kissing him. That was just one of countless things he would always miss.

Kelly was afraid that if Anna's photo was on display too much, it would become part of the forgettable things in the world. If he kept it out of sight until he was ready to fall asleep, and put it away soon after he awoke, she could spend the night with him and be there when he awoke.

This was Kelly's ritual and it kept him sane. Not happy or content, but able to cope. He stepped down from his camper into the mist and ran three miles, which was more than usual.

Evelyn Benson began her day as she did every day since her husband had passed away seven years ago. She collected his robe from the top of the bedspread next to her and picked up his worn slippers from the floor. She put them away in the closet where they would be until it was time to go to bed that night. Then she went downstairs to the little kitchen and made two cups of coffee, sipping one and letting the other go cold.

A knock on the door startled her and she leaned forward to peer around the antique hutch to see who it was. Maria waved at her through the glass in the front door. Their eyes met and Eve motioned for her to come in. Maria already had her copy of Eve's key in the door and she jiggled it skillfully, turning the old lock tumblers and freeing the stubborn latch.

"Morning. Thought you'd want to go on my rounds with me today. I've got a sick mare to see up in Davenport and we could swing by the café afterwards and have an early lunch," said Maria, checking the pot to see if the water was still hot. Maria Esteves was one of the few veterinarians in the area still making house calls. She liked to treat livestock, preferring them to miniature poodles and pampered cats.

"What time do you have to be there? I'm not ready to go anywhere, in fact I'm barely awake," replied Eve.

"No problem, I have to stop by the clinic and pick up some syringes and vaccines before I hit the road. I've got a lot of inoculations to give on my rounds. I could be back in a while to pick you up. Gonna be going all the way up to Pescadero today. Could use the company."

"I can go. It'll do me good to get out of the house. What's the weather forecast?" Eve asked, as she looked out the kitchen window.

"Windy. There's a couple of storms coming this way. It's likely to be rainy for the next two weeks. I'd bring some extra layers," replied Maria. Her weathered face told the tale of a life spent outdoors.

"Okay. I'll be ready by nine," said Eve. She smiled at Maria and watched her grind some coffee beans, toss the fresh grounds into a filter and pour hot water over them. No one else made herself as comfortable in Eve's home as Maria. Eve found that comforting. It made her feel like she didn't live alone. Eve and Maria had exchanged house keys just after Will had passed away. Either woman would drop in on the other unannounced for any reason, and for no reason. They called themselves the S.B.C: Sisters By Choice.

"Have you had any more dreams about Will lately?" asked Maria as she stood by the counter waiting for the water to pour through the grounds. She glanced over and saw a second coffee cup set out in memory of Will.

"A short one last night. It was very peaceful. Very nice."

"Did he talk to you?"

"No, he just smiled. I got the feeling that he just wanted me to be happy and go ahead with things."

"I'm sure he'd want that. It's strange that you get these dreams on the anniversary."

"Not strange. I start thinking about him, I look at old pictures, I close my eyes with his image in my mind and when I fall asleep the movie starts. I know it's not him, Maria, I know that. I'm not going psycho again."

"Do you feel okay otherwise? Depressed? Anything like that?"

"No, Doctor, nothing like that. In fact I'd like to go out tonight and hear some music. You know, have a few glasses of wine. Get crazy."

"Get crazy?" Maria laughed.

"Yeah, get crazy. Go way over the top. Maybe even order some onion rings and a cheeseburger. You know, *like wild.*"

Maria rolled her eyes. "Oh girl, now you're scarin' me."

"I've got a copy of the Good Times here. Let's check the club listings and see who's playing in town tonight," said Eve, moving Will's cup and motioning for Maria to sit at the table.

Maria slid into the chair and opened the paper to the entertainment section of the Good Times and scanned the listings. "Eek a Mouse is at the Catalyst. That's good reggae."

Eve shook her head.

"Vincent's Ear is at Moe's Alley."

"Too loud," said Eve. "What about the Bluebird? Who's there?"

"Kelly's back. That's all, just Kelly. Or maybe Kelly's back is the name of the band. Vincent's Ear, Kelly's Back, and Big Joe's Thingy. Which one do you want to see?"

"Big Joes' Thingy?! Where's he playing?" asked Eve.

"I just made that up to see what you're interested in."

"Funny."

"Well, it was funny!"

"Yes, Maria, it was funny. What's Kelly's back? Is back capitalized?"

"No, it's not capitalized. Ever heard of him?"

"Nope. Read what it says about him," said Eve.

"Kelly is back with the songs that made him a legend, and a bunch of new ones too. This guy is the real deal; a traveling musician with a story to tell. Great originals, smooth vocals, jazzy-blues guitar work and three decades of road dust. A must see. Your Best Bet for Friday night."

Eve raised her eyebrows, "The Good Times gave him 'Best Bet'?"

"Yeah, they did. Here's a picture of him. He's pretty cute for having 30 years of road dust on him." Maria handed the paper to Eve.

8

"Maybe he took a bath for the photo," said Eve.

The women laughed. Eve took the paper and glanced at the photo. She stopped laughing and lifted the picture for a closer look. The shot showed a tall slim man sitting on a rail fence with a guitar across his knee. His hair appeared medium toned in the newsprint photo, probably gray and brown, and his eyes were bright and piercing. *A rugged handsome face. A very handsome face*, thought Eve.

"Is he your type?" asked Maria.

"He's got a look about him that I like. Kinda fragile, even though he looks strong on the outside. He looks like he's been through some tough times. Maybe he lost someone."

"Geeez, you can tell that from a 3-inch black and white newspaper photo? Maybe we should go see him," said Maria.

"Why not? No one ever bothers us at the Bluebird, and they have good salads."

"Wait a minute. You said you wanted to get wild, have a cheeseburger, meet a man."

"The Bluebird has cheeseburgers, and you said the part about meeting a man, not me." said Eve, looking at the photo one more time.

Maria smiled and drained her coffee mug. "Okay, the Bluebird it is. We better get a move on. I'll drop by the office, get my stuff and be back here shortly. If I don't encounter any disasters today, we should be back by five. That gives us enough time to change and be there before the music starts. What are you gonna wear?" asked Maria.

"Something slinky, I mean slinky for that place. Probably black pants and my scoop neck top," said Eve. It was

9

her most revealing top and on the rare occasions she wore it, men forgot to look at her face.

"The secret weapon top?" asked Maria.

"That's the one."

Maria chuckled and headed for the door.

"What are you gonna wear?" asked Eve.

"I'll probably just go bare-ass naked, so I don't get ignored," she said as she stepped through the front door, turning for a last grin at Eve.

Eve smiled and waved goodbye. She picked up the newspaper after Maria had closed the door. She read the caption again, pausing to think about the part that said, *'a traveling musician with a story to tell.'*

She laid the paper down, collected the cups from the table and emptied them one by one into the sink. First the last drops of Maria's coffee, then her own, and lastly Will's cup, from which he hadn't taken a sip in seven long years.

Chapter Two

"What do you think?" asked Maria.

Eve played with her salad but neglected to bring any of it up to her lips. "About what?"

"About your salad."

"I think he's, well, interesting." Eve kept her eyes on Kelly, making no effort to turn and face Maria.

While Eve studied Kelly as he sat on a bar stool and sang, Maria studied Eve. It was the first time she'd seen her friend show so much interest in a man since Will had died. Maria found it fascinating. It reminded her of a movie scene of people under the influence of truth serum. She tested her theory.

"Is he handsome?"

"Yes."

"Do you think he's kind?"

"Yes, he's kind. He knows pain, and he would not want to hurt anyone."

"How can you tell?"

Eve turned and faced Maria. "Can't you tell? It's obvious. Listen to his voice. He's asking for someone in every sentence." Eve turned back to the stage.

Kelly was starting a slow shuffle blues tune. He leaned into it slightly and rocked his head to the beat. Conversations stopped and heads turned toward the stage, as the patrons strained to hear the soft guitar licks. The anticipation cut right through to Eve's core, and she gave him her full attention. Kelly began to sing in low tones, breathing into the mic.

Maria's attention shifted from Eve to Kelly. *He was not bad looking*, thought Maria, but it was his voice that she found most interesting.

While Kelly's voice interested Maria, it was intoxicating for Eve. There was a smooth quality to his tone, keeping it silky and expressive even in the passages when he strained for a high note or ground out a low phrase. She'd noticed that his eyes were gray with a hint of blue, but he kept them closed most of the time when he sang. She wished he would open them so she could read what he was feeling. This attraction was a new sensation for her and she was both confused and excited by it. Eve had never fawned over a musician before.

It was harmless, she told herself, and decided to enjoy the feeling. She unabashedly studied Kelly, feeling safe because he couldn't see her. *What was it about this man that was so fascinating?* His hair had been brown, but now it was more than half gray. He needed a haircut, there was no doubt about that, but the carelessness that he displayed by having his ears and forehead partially covered lent an honesty to his appearance that conveyed a lack of vanity.

He was thin by present standards and tall too. He looked like a man that worked the land, except his hands were clean and delicate. He moved them over the neck of the guitar with a relaxed purpose. There was an economy of effort in his every movement, even the tapping of his foot. His energy was devoted to his voice, and that was why Eve returned to his face.

The ridge of his narrow nose was deeply tanned, as were his cheeks. He was clean-shaven and it suited him well, because he had a strong square chin. *This man looked very different than Will,* thought Eve. Suddenly as Eve was staring at him, he opened his eyes. He was looking right at her and her heart raced. She held his gaze, more out of surprise than defiance. They looked at each other for a long moment as he ended the song. The audience applauded loudly, and he looked away to acknowledge them. Eve exhaled and settled back into her chair.

"He's pretty good, isn't he?" asked Maria.

Eve nodded in agreement. She lifted her wine and looked at him over the rim of the glass. He was waiting and they locked gazes again. Instinctively Eve touched the single pearl on the gold chain around her neck, covering the skin that was exposed by her low-cut top. His eyes didn't waver from hers, and it was her that broke contact.

"Are you warm?"

"No, but you are," replied Maria.

"No, I'm not."

"Eve, he's looking at you and you feel like you're under a heat lamp."

"What makes you say that?"

"Because you just twisted your pearl out of its setting."

Eve felt the loose pearl between her fingers. "It was ready to fall out. I was lucky to catch it." She let it roll into the palm of her hand and she closed her fingers over it. Stealing a sidelong glance at the stage she saw the empty chair behind the microphone and relaxed her grip. "I have some glue at home."

"Do you want to leave now and fix it?"

"No, let's stay for another set."

Eve returned alone on the following night, hoping Kelly would introduce himself to her on the break, but he was busy selling CDs and talking to fans. He looked her way, smiled and shrugged, indicating he was pinned down. She didn't want to appear as just another admirer, so she left after he got back on stage.

The day after that, she went to her hair stylist and also bought a new secret weapon top that was less revealing and more casual. On Kelly's third night at the Bluebird Café it was quieter. At his first break he quickly set aside his guitar, stepped down from the stage, and asked to join her.

"I was hoping you'd come back tonight. I really wanted to meet you," said Kelly. He extended his hand to her, palm up. She set her hand upon his and he gently closed his fingers. "Thanks for showing up," he said in whisper.

Eve had no verbal response. She smiled at him.

Chapter Three

In his dream, Kelly was lying on his back in a peaceful meadow, nestled under a soft blanket with his bare arms exposed to the warm morning sun.

Birds chirped loudly, driving him from his dream. He didn't open his eyes, preferring instead to stay in the partial sleep state that was half in the meadow and half in the present.

The smooth sheets against his skin and the pleasant aroma of a woman reminded him that he was in a bedroom, warm and safe from the chill outside. Beyond his eyelids, which he kept closed, the world was already in motion, reacting to a bright sun that hadn't been seen for two long weeks. The break in the weather was something he'd been dreading. His last two weeks with Eve had been glorious. Clear skies meant he'd be leaving his newfound, soon-to-be ex-lover.

Playing music for a living required a lot of farewells. People are often glad to see Kelly, but after a few weeks, he's played all his songs, told every story he can remember and eaten all the dishes on the menu. Then it's time to leave. Either he's saying good-bye to people that want him to stay or getting the cold shoulder from folks that want him to go. Either way, there comes a time when Kelly has to get in his truck and drive away.

Kelly had been drifting in and out of towns along the west coast for twenty-five years. Many people would call that a 'perpetual vacation', and when he thinks about the first seventeen years, he'd agree with them. During those years he was with Anna, his partner in life and love. Sadly, time is like wet snow, and each new layer crushes whatever lies below it. Seventeen years of glorious wandering are now under an avalanche of time. The memories aren't gone, they've become sweeter in the process; compressed, concentrated and sacred.

Anna and Kelly had all the beaches, parks and secret camping spots as their playground. It was easy to pretend they owned the coasts of California, Oregon and Washington. They had a home too, with a yard, nice furniture, and closets full of clothing. Everything seemed like a bargain because money flowed in faster than they could spend it.

Then Anna confided that a bump on the side of her breast had appeared and she was worried about it. She didn't want to make it into a big deal because they had no medical insurance, but Kelly insisted they go to a doctor. She was brave, the specialists were good and the couple threw every cent they had into the fight, but eight months and two operations later Anna died.

That's why Kelly's years of traveling the west coast are two starkly different chapters. The plush comfort of the bed he lay in with Eve asleep next to him resembles the first seventeen years. The tactile softness, the hint of perfume, and the penetrating warmth passing to the core of his body are sensations like a foreign language he once knew, but now has trouble speaking.

The cold vinyl seat of his truck and the foam mattress of the camper are elements from the last eight years. This more recent chapter is a part of Kelly's life that he tries not to think about. It's a part of his life that began as a shedding of possessions and became a self-imposed exile. There are times when his feeling of self worth is so diminished, he's surprised to see himself appearing life-size in the mirror.

Kelly had come full circle. He began the day with a dream. He awoke, knowing that his surroundings were as wonderful as his dream, and now he had to leave. It was his fiftieth birthday. That morning, Kelly's technique for peeling myself away from a situation wasn't working.

In response to his longing, the birds increased the volume of their chirping. Hidden in their cacophony he picked out individual notes from a classical melody. He thought back to a time that preceded his eight lonely years and the seventeen beautiful years with Anna. An earlier time that he rarely visited.

Kelly was six years old, watching a giant of a man dressed in navy blue overalls single-handedly hauling a piano out of his delivery van. He pulled it up onto the porch and into the family's little bungalow-style house. Kelly and his parents lived near the beach in Carmel, California where the smell of the ocean still lives in his memory. The man eased the piano

16

*through the front door and positioned it against the wall. Kelly's
mother sat down on the bench and carefully placed her delicate
fingers onto the keys. At first, she made no sounds, just gently
moving her fingertips over the snow-white ivory and smiling to
herself. Then, she pressed a finger down, then another, and in
seconds the room was filled with music. The song was 'Fur
Elise'.*

*The melody shimmered in the air and made the room
come alive. The tones expanded like the fragrance of fresh
flowers. Kelly must have heard a piano before, but this time he
was stunned by how beautiful and powerful it felt. The sounds
spilled over into all of his senses, as if he could feel, taste and
smell the music.*

*He touched the keys randomly as his mother played and
sensed that some notes were sour like lemons and others were
sweet like candy. His mother slowed her playing and
encouraged him to join in, watching closely as he pressed the
keys. In a matter of minutes, Kelly had the melody under his
fingers.*

*His mother left him on the piano bench and phoned a
music professor she knew from the college in Monterey. He
gave lessons and recitals, and she'd seen him perform many
times. She spoke with him briefly, explained what her son was
doing on the piano and the professor came over the next day to
test the boy's skills.*

*In six months Kelly was performing Bach Two Part
Inventions at a piano recital in Monterey. Two years later, at*

age eight, he was the featured performer at the annual Christmas Gala for the San Francisco Conservatory of Music. At age 19 he won first prize for Piano Performance at the Mozart Festival in Zurich, Switzerland. At Age 21 he took the Gold Medal in Moscow, the international pinnacle of classical piano performance.

After the competition he was the guest of honor at the gala dinner reception where the Minister of Culture of the Soviet Union placed a medal around his neck and kissed both his cheeks in front of an audience of a thousand dignitaries and famous musicians.

Twenty-nine years, and five thousand performances later, Kelly lay next to a woman he'd met while playing guitar and singing at a local tavern. An eighty-dollar-a-night gig. The ancient rust-spotted truck sat outside, sulking in the cold, waiting for him to start it up and point it north.

Moscow, Vienna and New York were buzzing with excitement, continuing to feed on the newest musical sensation, but Kelly was a universe away from them now. Decades had passed since placards with his photo sat atop easels in the lobbies of great concert halls. Kelly's parents, whom he had supported by playing for so many years, were resting in a cemetery, protected from seeing how their child prodigy was using his musical gifts.

It was bad enough that they had to see him abandon the piano, take up guitar, and start a rock band. The fact that his band enjoyed many commercial successes including four number one records, a Grammy, and several years of touring, didn't ease the disappointment they felt about their son's career choice. In some ways it was fortunate for them they died before he lost his grip on his rock career too.

Kelly cursed the birds and their chirping. He cursed them for taking him back to a golden time and then dumping him into the present. He wished they could work together to play a simple song that made sense, but they wanted to mock him. Kelly sat up in bed, feeling the skin of his nakedness press deeper into the sheets. Pushing back his hair, he looked down at Eve.

She knew nothing of Kelly's past. He was just a guy that played at the Bluebird in Monterey where she came with her friends once in a while. She noticed that he was better than any of the other acts, but that's as far as her knowledge went. If he'd mentioned that he'd been a headliner on the piano concert circuit she may have classified him as a delusional nut case and never become involved with him. And the rock career? He hadn't mentioned that either.

She was on her stomach with her face turned towards him. Her soft brown hair lay gently across her cheek, covering all but her eyelid, brow and forehead. Kelly hardly knew her, and he told myself that he didn't love her. How could he? They'd only met two weeks ago, and after all, she was just another woman that he'd had an affair with. Not Anna. Certainly nothing like Anna. These were the things Kelly said to himself to make the leaving easier.

He tried unsuccessfully to push everything about their courting experience to the back of his mind; the intriguing conversation at their first encounter, making a date to meet for breakfast the next morning, spending the rest of the day together, realizing that it was late and rushing to get to the gig at the Bluebird Café by 8 PM. Time had been absent on their first day together. The last two weeks had passed in a single moment. There was no time left. The leaving must begin.

Kelly constructed a mental image of Anna and placed it over Eve's sleeping form. Of course, he knew it would never fit and that was his reason for doing it. It was a trick he used to confirm that the woman he had slept with was a pretender. He'd done it many times in the last eight years. Afterwards he was stuck with the image of Anna, but he didn't mind that. Kelly's memory of Anna was a lifeline to him.

He slipped silently out of bed and headed for a hot shower. A vigorous scrubbing was a good way to change one's mood. Showers in truck stops, trailer parks, college campuses and shelters were not the same as a shower in a private home. Taking a sponge bath in his camper with a hot kettle of water was a distant third to the first two, but that's what he did to avoid going a day without bathing. Since he'd been staying with Eve, he'd taken two hot showers a day. He was tempted to shower three times a day, but that would have appeared excessive.

This stop in Monterey was similar to dozens of other episodes over the last eight years; a chance meeting, some

20

conversation, a lowering of defenses, and finally a sharing of intimacy. But Eve made him wonder if he'd been numb to the other casual affairs he'd had. In her presence he could taste the spice in his food and smell the sea on the wind. Kelly couldn't pinpoint the moment where the dreaming stopped and the waking began, but he was awake and he had been asleep.

It wasn't prompted by any questions she asked him, because she didn't question him like the other people who brought him into their homes. It was her kindness that disarmed him. She had a smile that could melt a glacier and the way she kissed his cheek before she fell asleep dissolved him completely.

Eve and Kelly had a few things in common. They were both trying hard to preserve what had once been attractive bodies, they were widowed, they had no children and they were unattached from the society at large; no regular jobs and no pressing obligations. But that was all Kelly could put into their list of similarities. Their differences were massive in comparison.

Eve lived in a cozy little house and Kelly lived in a camper. Eve had neatly folded cloth napkins and real silver utensils for every meal, even snacks. Kelly usually ate his food from the wrappers it was served in. Eve ground fresh beans for morning coffee by hand with her grandmother's Wedgewood grinder and carefully steamed the milk in a copper handled vessel. Kelly poured boiling water over grounds and didn't even wait for the grit to settle to the bottom before drinking it.

It wasn't that Kelly had never used silverware or drank wine from Viennese crystal before. Between the ages of 17 and 25, he'd lived in fine hotels all over Europe, taking all of his meals under the glow of chandeliers. When he was touring with his rock band they went through money like water. Later, when Anna and Kelly hit the road, they explored chic restaurants from Los Angeles to Vancouver.

The difference was that Eve's life had slowly evolved into a graceful elegance that she enjoyed maintaining. She treated herself well because she was at ease with how she'd gotten there. On the other hand, Kelly had been to a high place and fallen from it. Where she drew comfort from the sparkle of a gold-rimmed serving dish he was uneasy with it. Kelly feared his fingerprints would never wash off her wine glasses.

These impressions confused him. They brought up thoughts he'd buried under miles of asphalt from endless driving. If Eve had chattered on about senseless things like most other patrons, Kelly would have been busy answering questions or trying to tune her out. That didn't happen. Conversations with Eve were like time spent on a still lake. The ripples of their conversation were never frequent enough to make the water choppy.

Kelly reached for the hot water and turned it up until it started to burn. He began scrubbing his hair again for the second time, trying to distract himself, but he failed.

Eve was forty-four. She'd told Kelly that he had made her feel like no man had since her wedding night. He wondered if she'd said that to push a button in him and make him reply with a similar confession. Kelly hadn't said anything in return, but probably should have. What harm would it have done to return a compliment? But the fact was, she hadn't made him feel like his wedding night.

Kelly's wedding night with Anna existed in his memory as a spiritual experience. It was the feeling of belonging to someone that stuck with him. Anna and Kelly had been sleeping together for a year before they got married, and he remembered the details of their lovemaking from many of those previous nights. But the night they were married wasn't about sex. He didn't want to stain a perfect memory by pretending it had been duplicated.

Kelly had, admittedly, found himself in possession of more stamina than usual, but chalked it up to lots of sleep and Eve's home-cooked meals. Eve was an extraordinary cook. Perhaps she was sexier than any of the women he'd encountered in the last couple of years. After all, Kelly was fifty and the propositions had become less frequent and a lot less youthful.

Eve was good at a lot of things that could entice a wanderer his exit. Her nurturing spirit thrived on caring for any sparrow with a broken wing, which is probably what drew her to Kelly. She'd told him that men who wander need help.

Kelly knew in his heart that once he let his guard down and gave in to her creature comforts he'd be unable to control his cravings. Very soon he'd be buying new shoes, pricing a new truck, making plans for Saturday night, and then he'd get slapped down. Slapped down because he wouldn't have enough money to do everything he wanted.

Slapped down because he was too old and out-of-date to get a recording contract and slapped down because the woman he adored would either leave him or die.

It wasn't easy being a drifter, but it was a hell of a lot safer than taking your beating heart out of your chest and handing it to someone for safekeeping. The low life is the safe life. No one ever died by falling out of a basement window.

The loss of Anna started with a spreading numbness and turned into a gut-wrenching pain. Week one after Anna was gone was tolerable, week two was bleak, and by week ten he was spending full days in his sleeping bag clad in the same clothes he'd worn for days.

Kelly missed gigs, his house went into foreclosure, his possessions went into storage and the camper that had been a fun way to travel between performances became his home. Then the payments on the storage space became a hassle. One day Kelly went there to select a few things, leaving the rest for the management to haul away. The urn with Anna's ashes and the framed photo of her became Kelly's most important possessions. The paintings, photo albums, love letters, clothes, family antiques and fancy dishes; a history told in trinkets, were left for the scavengers.

Kelly took the urn with Anna's ashes to the beach. Standing on a rocky point above the Pacific Ocean, where they had stopped often in their travels, he opened the urn and turned

24

it upside down. Instead of having the wind take the contents out to sea, it suddenly changed and blew it right back onto him. On that day, years ago, her ashes coated Kelly like a glove. He could touch, but he couldn't feel.

Now, in the shower in Eve's home, he stopped scrubbing himself because he felt his skin getting raw. Kelly was truly clean, but the glove, the ashes, the invisible film remained. The water was getting cold and he rinsed off one more time. The bathroom was thick with steam, and he opened the window a crack to get the air flowing.

"You don't have to sneak away, Kelly, I'm not gonna chase your truck down the street," said Eve from the bedroom.

Kelly slipped his head out of the bathroom.

"I wasn't sneaking out, I was just being quiet," he said.

Eve was standing by the bed with her robe on and her hair brushed back. She didn't look mad.

"You look good, Eve," he said.

"Thanks. I'll make some breakfast and a bag lunch for you," she replied, suppressing a smile.

Kelly emerged from the bedroom to a kitchen filled with the aroma of strong coffee, bacon, and eggs.

Maybe Eve might throw a bucket of kindness at him to entice him to stay. Perhaps her plan was for him to open up his heart and pour out his sad story.

Although she hadn't asked Kelly to recount his history to her, it didn't mean she wasn't curious about it.

Why else would she be so nice to him on the day she knew he was leaving? Leaving was going to be hard, but staying would, in the end, be harder.

25

"You think your truck will start?" she asked, as she loaded up two plates with hashed browns, fresh ranch eggs, a Belgian waffle and five strips of bacon.

"I've only been here two weeks," he said.

"Well, it'll probably be okay then. That's not very long. You want some hot sauce?" She was starting out casual, but Kelly was sure there was a tempest brewing inside her. She brushed her light brown hair away from her pale green eyes as she stood by the fridge and waited for his answer. The soft north light from the window fell onto her face, splitting her fair complexion into cream and lighter cream.

Kelly looked down and spoke his answer to the plate. "If there's any of that pineapple salsa you made, I'll take that."

"I put the last jar into your care package. You want some catsup instead?"

"Okay," he replied. *She put the last jar into my 'care package'*, he thought. Nice touch. He shoveled a fork load of fried egg into his mouth so he wouldn't have to respond. The leaving always made an icebox out of the warmest house. If Eve wasn't going to make it cold, Kelly would, if that's what was needed to make a clean break.

"Great breakfast," he said, trying to be casual.

She looked up, winked at him, and started eating.

She's smooth, real smooth, thought Kelly. He let a few minutes elapse to give her some time to begin her appeal, but she kept eating and continued the silent treatment.

"What are you gonna do today?" He asked, helping her to get started. Kelly knew she was probably going through a difficult time. He was.

"I'm going to New York with my sister, Jeannie."

"I didn't know you had a sister."

"I've got two. Jeannie's two years older and Mona is a year and a half younger. Mona lives in upstate New York."

"Isn't it cold there now? Why don't you go in the summertime?"

"I miss the snow and I didn't get there last Christmas. The main reason I'm going now is because Jeannie's having her class reunion and I know more people from her class than my own. I want to see my mom too. She's gonna be seventy this week."

"That'll be nice. Did you just decide to go?"

"No, we've had our tickets for a couple months. You get the best prices when you book in advance. Especially from California."

"Yeah, I guess you're right."

She had her tickets for a couple of months, he thought. *Right. How did it happen that her ticket to leave was on the same day that he had decided to go? He guessed that if he decided to stay, she'd cancel her flight and be happy to avoid an expensive fare that she probably hadn't even booked yet. It wasn't an issue though, because the weather had cleared and he was heading north.*

"You know what I said about how you made me feel?" she asked.

Here it is. She's clever and she's cool, but she's caving in.

"Yeah…"

"And you know how you told me that I'd made you feel more active than you had for years?"

"Yeah…"

"Well I meant what I said, Kelly, but I wasn't talking about my 'level of activity'. I wasn't talking about the way either one of us performed. I wasn't thinking about what we did as if it was a sporting event. I don't have sex for that reason, and I've never met someone and slept with them right away like I did with you.

"I was talking about the way you made me feel. Inside. Inside here," she said, tapping a finger to the place between her breasts where her heart was beating. "You're a good human, a heck of a fine musician, and the most affectionate man I've been with since Will died seven years ago. I wanted to say that to you because life is unpredictable and we may never see each other again. Do you understand what I'm saying?" She wiped her mouth with a linen napkin, reached across the table for his hand and smiled. Kelly took her hand in his and squeezed it.

"Yes, Eve, I do understand. I've been traveling alone for eight years and I'm not used to treatment like this. The kindness and the honesty, I'm confused by it. I, well, I know this is different. You know what I mean."

"I think I do."

The conversation wasn't going exactly how Kelly imagined it would. Eve wasn't asking him to stay. She squeezed his hand again, and started collecting the dishes while she glanced at the clock. Kelly took his suitcase and guitar out to the truck, put them in the front seat and started the engine. The cursed thing cranked into life on the first try. He left it idling and came back into the house.

"Eve?"

"I'm in the bathroom, just getting into the shower. Come on back." She was standing next to the counter with a towel wrapped around her. The tiny bathroom was filling with steam again, making her seem like a misty vision from an old photo.

"Weren't you gonna say goodbye?" he asked.

"I thought you were just gonna drive away. I don't know how you leave, Kelly. I'm not very experienced, I told you that."

"Eve, I've learned more about you in the last thirty minutes than I did in the last two weeks."

"You've been paying a lot of attention this morning. Let me turn off the hot water." She leaned into the shower and turned the knob, catching her towel as it came loose. She wrapped herself up again and sat on the edge of the counter. Kelly came forward and started undoing the towel but she stopped him.

"Kelly, don't make this difficult for us. You've helped me turn the corner on my opinion about men and I've given you some tender loving care. Now the weather has changed, you're headed north, and I've got to get ready to take a trip. If we make love now it won't be as good as last night, and I don't want that in my mental scrapbook."

Kelly let his hand go from the towel and took her in his arms, kissing her cheeks, forehead and lips.

29

"You make me feel good about life, Eve. If I'm ever able to love someone again, I hope to God it's someone as kind and beautiful as you."

"Thanks, Kelly, that's a nice thing to say."

"When I come back this way, can I stop in and see you?"

"I'll be moving from here soon. It's time. This was where it all ended for Will. I did everything I could, but some things can't be stopped. One day he didn't wake up. After he passed away, his spirit stayed here for a long time. Now his spirit is gone and there's nothing to stay for. I called the landlord and told her I'll be moving in a month. I won't be here when you come through again Kelly."

"Oh."

"There's a hole in the maple tree out front. I'll put my new address in there."

"Put it in a matchbox and then dip it in wax a few times to seal it up. Otherwise the weather will get to it."

"Like a time capsule."

"Buried treasure," he said.

"Kelly?"

"Yes?"

"Before you leave, would you mind telling me your first name. All I know is Kelly," she asked, pulling her face from his chest and looking up at him.

"My name is Kelly Jacobs."

"No."

"Yes, it is."

"That's the name of the band that recorded my sister's favorite song, 'Curious'."

"That was me."

"Come on, Kelly. What's your real name?"

"Eve, I've got no reason to lie. I wrote and recorded that song. My name was, I mean is, Kelly Jacobs."

"Was Kelly Jacobs?"

"Well, that's not my original name. That's the name I made up when I got a recording contract. I was born with a different name."

"Are you going to tell me your real name? No, let me guess, Mick Jagger?"

"Eve, I haven't even said my real name for so many years that I have to think to get it right. I was superstitious about it for a while when I read that some Native Americans never let strangers know their true names because it could endanger them. Leave them open to spells. Silly, isn't it?"

"A little. Will you trust me with it?"

"My name was, I mean my birth name, even though I haven't used it since I was 25 years old, is Jacob Kelayoff."

"Wow. That's a Russian name. You're not Irish?"

"No, never was. Russian Jew. I could show you how I throw up when I drink whiskey just to prove it."

"Jacob," she said, pushing him away so she could see his face. "It fits you. Jacob fits you. What did your wife call you when you were alone with her? Did she call you Jacob? Is that why you don't let people know your real name?"

"She called me Kelly. I was Kelly Jacobs when I met her and she never knew me as Jacob. All of my documents say Kelly Jacobs. I've been Kelly for a long time."

Eve wove her fingers into his hair and pulled his lips to hers. They held their kiss for a long time and neither wanted to let go, but she ended it by letting her hands drop to his shoulders and easing him away. There was finality to her gesture.

"Jacob?"

"Yes?"

"Thanks for loving me, thanks for singing to me and thanks for telling me your name."

"Eve... I..."

"Jacob, don't say anything more." She put her fingers to his lips. "Don't say anything. And especially don't say goodbye."

He took one last look at Eve, nodded, and walked out of her house. By the time he got to his truck he was crying. Kelly hadn't done that since Anna died.

His face was hot in the cold morning air and he wiped his brow. Kelly dropped the truck into gear and made himself drive away, but he didn't get far without having to pull over and wipe his tears away.

Chapter Four

Kelly rounded the corner at the end of Eve's street and made a left onto Mission, taking him towards downtown Monterey. He felt out of balance. Partly because it was 8:00

AM, an unusual time for a musician to be up, and partly because he hadn't been in the cab of his truck for two weeks. He was assailed by the unpleasant odor of exhaust, oil, bits of hidden food and a hundred other ancient smells. In comparison to the aroma of Eve's hair and what she'd just cooked for their last breakfast together, his 'home' was pathetic.

Kelly's mental horizon was tilting and he couldn't stop it. All of the feelings that Kelly kept tightly sealed were washing across the deck of his brain, creating a stew of mixed emotions.

Instinctively he felt the last two weeks had to be followed by a dreaded let down. The nicer the train, the worse the wreck.

Kelly needed to return to the place he'd been before Eve had asked if they could nestle together like spoons. Perhaps some cold nights and rude meals would force his mental furniture back into place. It had to be done.

He planned to head up the coast and be in Berkeley by early evening, where he could drop into The Freight and Salvage Coffee House and confirm his next performance date. Then he would drive up to to Maison Restaurant in Emeryville and visit his old friend Michael. Kelly was always welcome to play there for tips, a meal, and to sleep on a cot in Michael's back storeroom.

Maison Restaurant was one of only a few venues where traveling entertainers could spend the night. Those places were disappearing, as the owners retired or went out of business. Serial killers and slasher films had done a lot to destroy American hospitality.

A change in Kelly's perception of the world had happened too. Some towns had become strange or unfriendly and he didn't feel right camping out in them anymore. When he got feelings like that he'd get a room, or if he was low on cash, he'd find a shelter.

When Anna and Kelly were touring together they were treated to nice accommodations in the homes of middle class families. People encouraged them to meet their kids, come to dinner with them and stage home-concerts. One family always knew another family in a nearby town and they worked like that for over ten years. After Anna died Kelly tried to make the same circuit, but the patrons weren't as open to a single man. This was in spite of his efforts to remain well-dressed, clean-shaven and groomed. Kelly began accepting less and therefore expecting less.

On the rare occasions when people invited him to their homes, he was offered a couch, or a driveway to park the camper and the use of the shower in the morning. Patrons were now mostly young musicians wanting to know how to get started. That was what he kept an eye out for. That's how he broke the monotony of what had become solitary confinement.

Patrons were easy to spot because they stood around after they'd bought a CD, waiting for the crowd to thin so they could get a chance for some personal conversation. Very few of them remember the Kelly Jacobs Band. Lately a few young people had said they heard about him by listening to their parent's records.

He had never met a single person that knew of Jacob Kelayoff, the 'boy wonder of the concert stage.' He'd come dangerously close to telling Eve who Jacob Kelayoff was. He was thankful she hadn't asked any questions about his distant past. One fall from grace could be overlooked, but two are chronic.

Kelly pulled over in front of the Bluebird Café, only ten blocks from Eve's house. He'd been playing the Bluebird Café for almost twenty years, and in all that time he'd never asked Jack, the owner, for a favor. Before Kelly left town he wanted to ask Jack to put him on his calendar for a month in the fall, when he hoped to be coming south again. It was February and Kelly feared the next few months might be difficult, based upon his first twenty minutes away from Eve. He needed to have something to look forward to, and a month in Monterey was at the top of his list.

He shut the engine off and slumped in the seat. Jack lived above the Bluebird and Kelly guessed he was still sleeping. He wasn't ready to bang on the door and roust him so he folded his arms and thought back to the first night he'd seen Eve in the audience.

He had asked Jack about her.

"A regular customer," Jack said. "Likes blues and jazz. Comes here with her girlfriend once in a while and they order my best bottle of wine. Not bad, eh Kelly?"

Kelly didn't know if Jack meant she was good looking, or that it was nice to have a customer order his best wine. Jack was openly gay, but that didn't mean he couldn't comment on how a woman looked.

35

On the third night she showed up alone and Kelly played one of his best sets in a long time. On the break, Eve ordered coffee and stayed. Kelly introduced himself and asked if he could join her.

In their first twenty minutes, they talked about a host of subjects. The ozone layer, ice core samples from the Arctic, the migration of early man, communication, the guitar as a tool, how the human mind reacts to sound and other stuff; things that Kelly hadn't conversed about for years.

Behind her reserved demeanor, this woman has quite an intellect. What a gem, thought Kelly.

Then it was time for him to play another set. He suggested they pick up the conversation at breakfast the next morning and she agreed. In between two songs Kelly stopped to tune his guitar and when he looked up, her seat was empty.

Kelly was startled out of his memories by a loud tap on his window. It was Jack.

"Hey, Irish! I thought it was you," he shouted through the window. Kelly opened the passenger door and Jack slipped in and sat down.

"Are you heading up to the Bay Area? Steve at Freight and Salvage is looking for you. He wants to know if you're gonna make your gig on Friday night. You didn't call him."

"Yeah, I'll make it. Can you call him and confirm for me, my cell phone is busted."

Jack laughed. "You don't own a cell phone! What died in here?"

"Oh sorry," Kelly said, rolling his window down. "The cab's been shut tight for two weeks. I guess my compost pile of fast food under the seat is ready to be turned."

"I was thinking it smelled more like a decomposing transmission. What are you doing parked in front of my place at eight-thirty in the morning?"

"I wanted to ask about booking a month here in the fall. I've met some good players here and I think I could put together some great shows, mix it up a little to make it interesting. You know, like a mini festival."

"You got bit, didn't you Kelly?"

"Yeah, Jack, I guess I did."

"I kinda figured that was gonna happen when you started hangin' with her. Comin' in together and goin' home with your arm around her every night. Bites are dangerous at our age, Kelly," said Jack.

Kelly looked at Jack's face and read the lines of compassion. They were deep and dark. His thick gray eyebrows were lowered over his coal black eyes, which were studying Kelly to see the damage. Jack rubbed a calloused hand across his jaw and nodded his head sympathetically.

"You been bit lately?" Kelly asked.

"Not for a while. I'm seeing a graduate student now, and he's got another six months before he finishes up. He might stay, but they usually don't. He's twenty-seven and I'm fifty-three. It don't look good. How old is the woman?"

"Forty-four."

"And you?"

"I turned fifty today."

"No kidding? You look decent for fifty. Well, I'd say you've got a chance. She looked like she was nuts about you. And you sang every song right to her. Especially Visions of Anna. You don't do that one very often. It's hard to sing, isn't it?"

"You know it is, Jack."

"Yeah, I do. What's her name?"

"Eve."

"Nice name."

"Yeah."

"Geeez, Kelly," he said in a whisper, looking across the seat and shaking his head. "I didn't realize it was that serious. You really sang the hell outta that tune. You sang it like a starving beggar, if you don't mind me sayin' so."

"Oh no, not at all. It's just what I need to hear. Perfectly okay, Jack, really."

"Have you talked to Anna about her?"

"Anna is dead, Jack."

"I know that, you lame-brain. I know Anna is dead. She was the last woman you loved, wasn't she?"

"Is it that obvious?"

"Just to me. You gotta talk to her about this woman. Eve. You gotta make your peace. Even if it don't work out, you gotta let her know that you're ready to move on. You gotta talk to her."

"How do you know so much?"

"Because I watch and listen when other people are flappin' their jaws. And because I'm Romanian and my mother

38

and her mother and all the women in my family were palm
readers. I can tell you a lot about yourself, but it's better that you
learn it on your own. I'll give you a month in the fall. September
15th to October 15th, how's that? Then your name won't be
splattered across a whole page of my calendar. Who you gonna
play with?"

"Well, I haven't decided that yet."

"You don't have anybody in mind, do you, Kelly?"

"No, Jack, I don't."

"Okay, Irish, I'll bail you out 'cause I like you. I have a
bass and drummer I can throw into the mix for the first two
weeks. College kids, but good players. The last two weeks
you're on your own and you better make it good. Play a little
piano too. You used to play piano pretty good. Give me all your
material on CDs, and the charts if you've got 'em."

Kelly reached under the seat and pulled out four tapes
and two CDs.

"That's all of it, six albums. I don't have charts."

"Okay," Jack said. He looked anxious to be on his way.

"Hey, Jack?" Kelly said.

"Yeah?"

"Did you ever see Eve with any other guys, you know
like other singers? Did she ever go home with any other
musicians?"

"Nope. Never even seen her with a male date."

"Could I call you, you know, to see if she's been in the
Bluebird?"

"Geez, Irish, you don't even know how to drive a nail
anymore, do you? How did you leave it with her?"

39

"Pretty good, I think, but she didn't ask me to stay."

"Well, that may not be bad. She looked smart enough to know that you need a lotta asphalt in your diet, bein' a rover and all. Maybe she was just protecting herself."

"Yeah, maybe."

"Did you leave anything behind for her?" asked Jack.

"Like what? Like a present?"

"Geez, Irish, you're so dense! Did you leave a personal item with her? A token, a part of you?"

The only thing Kelly had left behind was his original name, but he didn't want to mention that to Jack. He wouldn't understand.

"No, I didn't leave anything behind."

"Yes, you did, it's written all over your face."

"Well…"

"Don't tell me about it!" Jack shouted. "Once you tell me, then it ain't personal anymore! Do what I said. Have a one-on-one with Anna. Do you know where her spirit is?"

"How would I know that?"

"There must be a place where you think about her every time you pass by it. A campground, a restaurant, a hotel, her gravesite…"

"Her gravesite. Well, it's the place I scattered her ashes. Up the coast between here and Half Moon Bay."

"Did you get any of her ashes on you?"

"Yeah. Why?"

"You'll need to do a spiritual bath there, to wash it off."

"But it happened eight years ago."

"You know, Kelly, you look smarter than you are. Did she have a favorite wine or drink?"

"She didn't drink much, but when she did, she drank Beefeater Gin."

"Get a big bottle of it. Stand naked and pour half of it over your head, then start talkin'. Don't worry about gettin' an answer, just say what your feelin' and don't be shy about apologizing, they like that. When you're finished, pour the rest over your hands and feet, and then take a bath. Salt water works best, if you can handle it. The Jews call it a mikvah, but they don't use a bottle of liquor. That's something added by the Romanians. You gotta do it, Kelly, if you ever want this thing with Eve to work out." Jack stepped down from the truck and turned to walk away.

"Hey Jack?" Kelly said again.

"Yeah?"

"Why did you say that I used to play piano? You've never heard me play piano."

"Kelayoff. Ke-lay-off." said Jack, as if he was talking to someone with a broken hearing aid. Then he slammed the door and walked away. Kelly followed him in the rearview mirror, watching him get smaller and smaller until he disappeared.

Kelly sat in the truck thinking about what Jack had said. The gin, the thing about being bit, the way he said Kelly sounded like a starving beggar, *and Kelayoff.* Jack knew.

Kelly had heard about the mikvah ceremony. His grandfather had explained it as a spiritual cleansing that should be done in either fresh spring water or a water source that's connected to the ocean. Kelly had never done a mikvah.

41

Hot flashes started again and Kelly rested his forehead against the steering wheel to calm himself.

Although Kelly had known Jack for nearly twenty years, he couldn't say he was a friend. He was a guy that always got right to the point and then moved on to other things. If you were in a conversation with him and the 'other things' didn't involve you, he'd walk away. It's hard to develop a deep friendship with someone like that. On the other hand, Kelly admired Jack's insight. He had shocked Kelly before with his powers of observation, but nothing like today.

Kelly bought a half-gallon of Beefeater's Gin at the market. It cost twenty-seven dollars, but he bought it anyway. There were cheaper brands, but Anna never drank the off brands. Kelly placed the bottle under the seat and started the truck.

Chapter Five

The way Kelly felt about Highway 1 was something like the way most people felt about the staircase in their home. Every step, every spot on the carpet and every nick in the handrail is familiar. In his mind's eye he pictured the bluff above the ocean where he had scattered Anna's ashes.

There were low lying chamomile plants nestled in the rocky soil and flowering lupine bordering the drifts of sand. The tracks of the Southern Pacific Railroad lay between the road and the steep switchbacks leading down to the beach. Halfway down the steep trail to the beach, just past the cluster of poison oak that Anna always warned him about, was a level spot to stand. From that place there was a fine view of the coast, looking north and south. That's where Kelly could talk to Anna.

The traffic thinned out and soon Kelly was alone on the highway. The previous evening's moist ocean air had left the road and all the foliage wet and glistening. Not far ahead he could see the highway leading into a fog bank. The picture of Anna's beach filled Kelly's mind. He knew exactly what it would feel and smell like when he got there.

Kelly thought about what Jack had told him, and tried to make a list of things he would say to Anna, but as the distance to her beach decreased, he decided to sing a few songs instead. No lyrics he knew seemed appropriate.

Kelly pulled off the road and parked in the spot he used every time he visited this beach. Jack had said for him to be naked when he spoke to Anna and he was thankful that it was early in the day when the fog was still thick enough to keep visitors away from the coast. There was a long overcoat in the camper, and he went back to get it, knowing that it would be the best thing to wear on the walk down to Anna's spot.

Kelly opened the camper door and stepped inside, closing it behind him. The curtains were drawn tight and it was dark, but he knew every inch of the small enclosure and stepped forward to the place where the overcoat was stored. Walking forward, his foot hit an unexpected object in the aisle and he tripped, hitting his head on a cabinet as he fell. In a second Kelly was down, dazed from the impact and rubbing the cut on his forehead. He opened a curtain for light to see how bad he was cut and what he'd tripped on. Just above his right eyebrow was a

43

deep and bloody gash. In the aisle was a small wooden box he'd never seen before.

Ignoring his wound Kelly picked up the case and examined it. It was very old and worn. Inside the case was the Wedgewood coffee grinder Eve had gotten from her grandmother. It had a small note attached.

Take care of yourself and thank you for helping me to open up. Love, Eve.

Kelly set the note aside, placed the case on the floor and stood up on shaky legs. He tried not to cry. He didn't want to cry because he was afraid that once he got started, he wouldn't be able to stop. Maybe he'd start crying at gigs when he sang songs about Anna. He didn't want that. Kelly squeezed his eyelids together as hard as he could so no moisture could leak out. He saw flashing colors because he squeezed so hard, but it didn't help. He hadn't taken a breath for a long time and when he gasped for air his eyes popped open and tears ran down his face.

With a bandage on his head, his guitar strung over his shoulder, a half-gallon of gin in hand and a wool overcoat covering his naked body, Kelly walked through the fog toward the trail to sing a song to Anna.

Chapter Six

Kelly crossed the railroad tracks and stopped at the top of the path. The storms had played themselves out over the last two weeks and now damp ocean fog sat on the day like milk.

Kelly could hear the cold salty waves lapping onto the shore long before seeing them.

On a clear day there would be an expansive view up and down the coast, but on this morning he couldn't even see six feet ahead of him. He stood still and listened to the sea birds landing on the water, chattering, and taking off again. There was an occasional car passing behind him and off in the distance a foghorn croaked. All of these sounds were intermittent, with long spaces of silence between them. Even the waves seemed to be waiting, listening, anxious to hear what he'd come to say.

Kelly continued down the steep path, occasionally slipping, but never falling. The going was difficult in the loose and crumbling shale, especially because he couldn't make out any familiar footholds in the fog. Kelly spotted the clump of poison oak on the right and knew he was getting near the bottom. Then the trail leveled out and he was standing on the plateau where he'd spread Anna's ashes. He couldn't see anything. Not the coast, not the water, not the sky. Anna and Kelly often stopped here for the view, but if it was foggy like today, they always walked to the water's edge. That's where Anna would be today, so Kelly kept going down the path.

After reaching the sand, Kelly trudged ahead toward the water. Finally reaching the wet sand, he could barely make out the water line only five feet away. He'd never seen fog this thick. Anna's spirit could be felt on the damp air.

There was a half-buried log in the sand, worn smooth from being washed out to sea and deposited again onto the beach. It was about four feet thick and forty feet long. It occurred to Kelly that it would take at least thirty years before it

45

broke into splinters, maybe more. Even though it had been toppled and dragged down a creek into the sea, it would end up sticking around on this earth longer than Kelly or anyone he knew. He sat on the log and placed the guitar in its familiar position across his right knee.

Kelly was in place and the world was listening, perhaps even Anna was listening, but he didn't know where to start. *This has to be a new song*, he thought. His fingers formed a minor chord on the guitar, and he began picking the strings.

"Dear Anna, dear Anna, dear Anna of my heart
May I, could I, would you, show me where to start?
I haven't lost my feelings for you, or forgotten how it was
You and I doing what a pair of lovers does
Since you left this world, I've been on a long descent
Now I want to climb back up, and I'm seeking your consent

Dear Anna, dear Anna, dear Anna of my heart
Things have been so hard since we've been apart
Your leaving, my dear Anna, was cruelly premature
And one day, someday, we'll be rejoined I'm sure
But just for a short moment, while I remain earth-bound
May I spend some time with a woman, that I've newly found?

It's nothing really, well Anna, that's not exactly true
But she's not of course, dear Anna, anything like you
She can help me, in ways, that you're now unable
I need the help of someone, to steady what's unstable

46

If angels have their feelings, I hope you feel no pain
I hope you understand what I'm trying to explain

Dear Anna, dear Anna, dear Anna of my heart
May I have permission to make another start?"

Kelly ended the song in a whispered voice. There was no answer. No hint of Anna's voice rode on the mist to tell him it was either permitted or forbidden to fall in love again. Despite that, he felt better than he had all morning.

The bottle of gin sat beside him in the sand and he knew it was time to have a drink with Anna. He took the first swallow, so she wouldn't be shy. He held the bottle out to the fog for a moment, but then set it onto his knee. Anna would never have taken a pull right from the bottle, that wasn't her style, so he carefully filled the cap and balanced it on the log beside him. This wasn't the first time Kelly shared a drink with a spirit.

When Kelly was young, his family had Passover dinners at his grandparents' home in San Francisco. There was always an extra place at the table and a glass of wine set aside for the Prophet Elijah. The front door was always left slightly ajar for Elijah, or any other Jew who had no table of his own. Kelly closed his eyes and thought back to the way he watched the wine glass intently to see if Elijah, who was presumably invisible, would take a sip. When his gaze was at it's most focused, his grandfather would always gently nudge the table and shout, "Yacob, did you see it?! Did you see the wine go down? Did you see Elijah take a sip?"

47

"Yes, Grandpa, I saw it," Kelly would say amid the stifled laughter of the family. He knew he was the object of a joke, yet upon close inspection it did seem as though the wine had indeed gone down slightly after the shaking stopped. Elijah had many houses to visit, grandfather reminded everyone at the table, and he couldn't be expected to take a full swallow at each one. Elijah was a wise and learned man.

The white plastic top of the gin bottle was filled to the brim and it teetered on the log. If Anna wasn't going drink it perhaps Elijah would drop by and knock a few back. *After all, he was off most of the year.*

Kelly set his guitar down on the sand and got up, taking great pains not to topple the cap over. He took off his coat and stood naked against the damp gray air. The chill of the morning did not cut through to his core as he'd expected. The hot breakfast and the warmth from his time with Eve had not yet left him.

The water was only a few steps away and Kelly waded in up to his knees. It was icy. Painful in fact, and it confirmed that even though he could tolerate the chilled air, he was not magically protected from the elements. Kelly took another gulp of gin, coughing most of it up in a spray. Then he tilted his head back and started pouring gin onto his forehead and shoulders. The liquid ran down his neck and back in clear rivulets, ending up in the salt water. Instinctively Kelly stepped out of the ocean back onto the sand. Gin, even good quality gin, was not good for the sea.

48

The cold air felt warm against his ankles, compared to the seawater. Kelly continued pouring the gin onto his arms, chest and back. Even in the cold air he could feel it evaporate, creating a stinging sensation. When the bottle was almost empty he took another swallow, managing to keep it down. Kelly checked the bottle cap to see if Anna or Elijah needed a touch up. Apparently they didn't drink in the morning. He poured the rest of the gin over himself and set the bottle down. His shivering had begun, and he dreaded what was yet to come.

Without hesitation Kelly ran forward into the ocean until his legs were tripped up in the deep water and he fell forward with a splash. The frigid Pacific was shocking, and his lungs felt as though they would burst. He found his footing with some difficulty and stood up with only his head and shoulders out of the sea. His attempts to breath resulted in fast shallow gasps. Just then Kelly was hit by a wave. It washed over him, and he thrashed furiously, not sure which way was up. He'd never struggled so hard as he did at that moment to reach the surface.

Suddenly Kelly's head popped up into a swirl of foam, and he saw the shore receding. He was being taken out to sea in the retreating wave and he made no progress trying to swim to shore. Another wave hit him from behind and he was lifted and carried toward the beach.

Kelly's arms and legs started moving instinctively. The water began receding again and he fought it fiercely. As he kicked and paddled, the sea was drawing away under him. In moments he found himself on his belly in the wet sand.

Another wave was coming. Kelly staggered toward shore on his knees. There was no feeling in his skin, even though the sand and rocks were cutting him. Between throwing up seawater, he managed a few gasps and started breathing. Kelly made it to his feet onto dry sand and sat on the log. Both hands shook uncontrollably and his teeth chattered loudly.

Using the outside of his long coat, he wiped off the water and rubbed his hair vigorously. Then he put the coat on and fumbled with the buttons, managing to get only three fastened. The relief of feeling his body heat trapped in the coat was reassuring. Almost at once his muscles became less tense and he was able to breath regularly. The shivering continued but didn't worsen. Kelly had completed the mikvah. It was just as Jack said. He felt different.

Kelly collected his guitar and the bottle, drinking the capful of gin on the way up the trail. In the camper he heated some water for coffee. Inside the little drawer of Eve's grinder Kelly found just enough grounds for a strong cup. He made the brew and drank it down, grit and all. Then he slipped into his sleeping bag and waited for his body to warm up.

Kelly's mind wandered over the events of the past few weeks. Eventually his thoughts came to the first time he'd seen Eve. She had come into the Bluebird Cafe with another woman and sat at a table close to the stage. Even in the dim light of the Bluebird her hair was soft and shiny, falling onto her shoulders. She chatted with her friend and didn't seem interested in the music at first, but midway through the third song Kelly caught her looking at him. They locked eyes and she turned away. That's when Kelly got his first good look at her.

She'd taken her coat off and he ran his gaze over the smooth pale skin of her face and neck. Her profile was girlish, with dimpled cheeks, small nose, and full lips. He let his eyes roam over her, knowing that she felt him staring at her. Kelly explored the bare skin below her neck that led down to the shadow formed by her cleavage. She certainly knew he was looking at her then and she turned toward him to confirm it. Their eyes met again, but this time it was Kelly who looked away.

He had just started a song called Visions of Anna. Like many of the songs he'd written over the last eight years, it was a lament. Kelly had forgotten how to write happy songs, and his muse, while not abandoning him completely, had seen fit to dole out the tunes grudgingly. A lyric here, a musical phrase there. The slow way in which his material was delivered made it impossible to assemble any of it into a quick tempo song.

In the years when he fronted the Kelly Jacobs Band, he got his ideas in flashes, sometimes writing an entire song in his head while relaxing on a hotel room sofa. Anna would come into the room and he'd ask her if she wanted to hear a new tune. He'd grab his guitar and play it for the first time, sounding as if he'd rehearsed it all day.

Kelly had much more material than the band needed in those days. The songs flowed from his muse to him and onto the pages of his notebooks. Most of the tunes were never performed on stage or recorded. Over the last eight years Kelly had settled into a somber mood for his originals, and it was Visions of Anna that he was singing the night when Eve and he made their first connection.

51

A Beggar's Tune

"When the lights go dim, and the neon dies
I lay myself to rest, and I close my eyes
My feet leave no prints, for the rain to wash away
Walking in my mind, I join with visions of Anna

"Across a bridge we know to be endless
Into a night where the moon never goes
Through a doorway that leads down a staircase
Beneath a world that lies sleeping and cold

"Day is a wall that keeps me from Anna,
 Night is a passage to the one that I love
She calls tonight across tall towers,
I play her song, she knows that I'm here

"I live for dreams, they keep me alive,
When I'm gone, there'll be no more Anna
No one knows the sweetness she brings
No one knows how precious she is

"I hope I live ten thousand more nights
I'll pay the price with ten thousand more days
Whatever it takes to bring me to Anna
Whatever it takes to make her my own

"The hour approaches, the crowd is thin,
I play my song so Anna can hear me

No one asks where I go after closing,
No one cares where the music man went
Only Anna   has a place in her heart
Only Anna   gives me her warmth

Only Anna"

When Kelly ended the tune, he got the scattered applause he'd come to expect after a ballad. Eve didn't applaud at first. She looked at him, silently wondering who Anna was and why she had to go? Kelly didn't just imagine this. She told him what she'd been thinking when they spoke of it later. She told him that Visions of Anna, even though it was sad, was one of the nicest ways anyone could be remembered. When she heard that song, she knew he was hurting.

As Kelly had learned, there's comfort to be found in loss. It doesn't present itself right away, and it doesn't offset the pain of loss, but the person left behind can find comfort in acknowledging how much the departed meant. That acknowledgement proves that the person being mourned was special. Furthermore, it's comforting to say out loud that you were loved by that person, even if the statement is woven into song lyrics. Eve understood that.

There was a lot in Kelly's music that resonated with Eve. She stayed until closing that first night and came back the next two nights. On the third night when they had their first conversation, it only took a few sentences to reveal why he was hurting. "My wife, Anna, died eight years ago."

Eve replied, "I lost Will seven years ago." That was all they needed to clarify their connection.

Kelly was getting warmer in his sleeping bag and more relaxed. He revisited his memory of Eve's face again from several different angles. It was the first time he'd dwelt on the face of a woman besides Anna's and it helped him to shed the chill of his ritual bath. Kelly soon drifted into a deep sleep. He lay dreamless and still for almost an hour. When he awoke he came to a realization.

He was free to do anything he wanted with the time he had left on this Earth, except waste it.

Chapter Seven

Kelly rolled up to the Freight and Salvage in Berkeley to check in with Steve. The Freight and Salvage is a Bay Area institution. It holds 87 people in folding chairs and another 15 at the coffee bar. When musicians get famous and draw large crowds, they regret they can't play at The Freight anymore. The Kelly Jacobs Band went through that period, but Kelly was past that now.

Steve was inside, loading beer into the cooler.

"Hey Steve, how are you?"

"Mr. Kelly Jacobs, live and in person! You look good, brother. You ready for Thursday, Friday and Saturday? It would be nice if you had a phone so we could confirm."

"Have I ever missed a date?" asked Kelly, shaking Steve's hand.

"No, Kelly, you're solid. You're solo on Thursday at eight. You're opening for Kit Wells on Friday and Saturday, so you need to start at seven."

"I've never opened for anyone here. Kit Wells opened for me here a few times," mused Kelly.

Steve looked at Kelly and nodded. "Kit is hot right now. Don't be bothered by that. You'll get there again." There wasn't any conviction in Steve's voice.

Kit Wells had been coming up when Kelly was nearing the top of his fame. Kelly knew Kit's brilliant singing and song writing would pay off one day, and those days had come. Fortunately, Kelly had followed the axiom, "Be nice to people on your way up, because you'll need their kindness on your way down." Kelly had been nice to Kit, and he needed a favor from him now. Steve gave Kit's number to Kelly.

"Hey Kit, this is Kelly Jacobs. How are you doin'?"

"Kelly! Long time, man. I'm doing well. We're on the bill together this week. I'm lookin' forward to that."

"Yeah, me too. Who you got playin' with you at the gig?"

"Ben Carter on drums and Kato on bass. You know 'em, right? Kato toured with you."

"I don't know Ben, but I'm sure he's good if he plays with you. Kato's a great player. I've got a favor to ask. You can say no and I'll understand. I'm just doing a single and I'm hoping that your guys can back me up towards the end of my set. It would help me. I've got some new material and it needs a bigger sound than just me on guitar."

"No problem, Bro. I can't speak for those guys, but I'm sure they would be happy to play with you. Got charts and recordings?"

"Well, Kit, the stuff is too new for recordings, but I can make some charts. If we did a session before the sound check, like an hour, I could get them up to speed. They have big ears."

"Okay, sounds good. I'll run it past them and call you back. What's your number? Your caller ID says your calling from the Freight."

"I don't have a cell phone. It got smashed and I need to get a new one. Why don't I call you tomorrow about this time?"

"Sure, man. We'll talk then."

"Thanks, Kit."

"You bet, Kelly."

Kelly hung up the phone and thought about where he'd sleep that night. He had a lot of work to do in four days, but no spare cash for a motel where he could hunker down and write music. The only new songs he had were sad ones, and none of those had charts. Kelly had song ideas, all of which has started bubbling up after his first night with Eve, but he was hours and hours away from being prepared. The cold ocean had jolted him into high gear. Now those songs were dancing in his head, anxious to get out.

In the next two days he wrote song ideas on his familiar yellow pad. The weather was clear and crisp, and he visited park benches and hiking trails where he'd written hit songs in the past. At night, with his camper parked on a service road in Tilden Park, far back in the Berkeley hills, he continued writing by candle light, never pausing to rehearse anything.

In the mornings he entered the locker room on the U.C. Berkeley campus. After his long hot showers, he sat in the campus coffee shop and wrote more.

Across the country:

During these days Eve took long walks on snow covered paths near her mother's house in New York. The familiar sights and sounds were pleasant, but not magnetic.

Be patient, she thought to herself. *Home will eventually take effect on me and I'll feel good about moving back.*

That was a good theory, but there didn't seem to be enough room in her mind for that to take hold because thoughts of Jacob took up all the vacant space.

The day of the gig, Kelly found a parking space right across the street and loaded up his pushcart with a couple guitars, his amp, and his tall stool with the worn out cushion. The close parking space was a good omen. It was going to be a fun night. That's just what he needed to take his mind off Eve.

Steve was there to help Kelly in. It was only 3 PM and the show was scheduled for 7.

"We'll get the piano moved off to the side for you as soon as the other guys show up. That thing gets heavier every year and I can't push it myself anymore."

"Leave it up there. I'm gonna play some tunes on piano tonight."

Steve raised an eyebrow. "You play piano?"

"A little."

"Kelly, you've been playing here, what, 30 years? You've done at least 50 shows here. Probably more. Never played piano in all that time. How '*little*' can you play? If it's not a *big little*, we're gonna move it out of the way." Steve looked away and continued putting pastries into the glass case.

Kelly turned and walked onto the stage. He pulled the piano bench out, sat down, lifted the cover, and exposed the keys. It had been a very long time since he'd sat at a quality grand piano. He placed his fingers onto the cold keys and moved them forward and back, careful not to press any of them down. He concentrated. With his eyes closed, he transported himself back to his final performance at the Moscow Piano Competition.

The hall was buzzing with voices and clinking glasses, but once he was in position, the entire room became absolutely silent. It was then that Jacob Kelayoff began with the first of three pieces required by the judges. Performers only knew which pieces they were required to play the day before their performance. The competition was in Moscow, and the judges were all Russians. They reserved the difficult pieces for foreigners, and the most difficult for the only American to get into the finals.

The first piece was Etude Opus 25 No. 6, by Chopin. At one minute fifty-four seconds, it's considered to be one of the most challenging concert piano pieces of all time. The young Kelayoff began the piece with the flurry of notes that set the tone for a lightening quick rendition. He was nervous and he knew that his quick tempo was going to make it nearly impossible to execute the complicated left hand counterpart without crashing, but slowing down would be the kiss of death. After a few bars, he abandoned his thoughts about tempo and slipped into a state of grace.

The judges looked at each other. One of them had started his stopwatch. Performers often started pieces too fast, and even if they finished without significant errors, rushing through a piece detracted from their scores. These judges were anxious to penalize an upstart American. Kelayoff had never studied with great teachers, or even studied in Europe at all. Where was Carmel, California, anyway?

Kelayoff powered through the piece with precise articulation, emotional control, and an interesting use of subtle dynamics. He finished after one minute forty-one seconds, one second within the acceptable parameters. Letting the last notes ring, he opened his eyes and blinked. The audience was immediately on their feet applauding. This was unheard of at the competition. A normally reserved Russian audience only clapped at the end of the third piece. Jacob Kelayoff turned slightly to the audience and gave them a subtle nod.

"That was great!" yelled Steve. "Unbelievable!!"

Kelly took a deep breath and stood up. He looked at Steve and gave him a half-smile, then walked off stage to the green room to sit quietly with his notebook and organize some of his song ideas into music charts.

By the time 6:30 rolled around for the sound check, Kelly had four songs sketched out. They weren't like the sad ballads he'd been writing since he'd lost Anna. He decided to play all of these new tunes on piano. He wouldn't have time to iron them out and rehearse them, so they'd be rough, but during his rock days he knew that rough was honest.

The crowd was big for a has-been like Kelly Jacobs. Real big for a Thursday night. As Kelly was tuning his guitar, Steve came up on the stage and knelt down.

"Jack from the Bluebird called me. He told me he telephoned the radio stations and asked them to put a plug in for you. That guy has pull. In fact, he just walked in with his boyfriend."

Kelly looked up and saw Jack and his friend taking a couple of vacant seats in the back. Jack made a motion to Kelly like someone pouring a bottle over his head. Kelly nodded and mouthed, "Thank you."

The night started out with Kelly telling a story about his experiences as the leader of a top rock band from nearly two decades ago. He made jokes about seeing his albums everywhere.

"In fact, just this morning I was at a garage sale in San Jose…" Kelly paused.

The crowd loved it.

"Now I know this wasn't billed as a retro concert, but I'm gonna play a few of my hit tunes. You know the ones I mean. They're getting a lot of play... in rest homes." He launched into the first tune.

The crowd was enraptured by the way Kelly attacked the material. He was slapping his guitar, doing fast and complicated licks, and singing with strong emotion. At the end of his first tune, the house burst into applause. He didn't wait for them to settle down before beginning again. He took a break after the fourth tune to set his guitar onto the stand and sit at the piano.

The crew adjusted the lighting and now Kelly was seating in the bright column of a yellow spot. He ran his fingers through his hair and looked at the place where his music notes should be. *I left them in the green room*, he thought to himself. That didn't matter. He'd just written the tunes and they were still floating on the surface of his mind. He was happy he had no music to read.

He began a steady boogie-woogie left hand groove. With his right hand, he reached over and swung the mic up to his lips.

Then without warning he shouted, "Hang on!" while both hands came crashing down on the keys. The sound stopped suddenly because he had stomped on the dampening pedal. The crowd was silent. A full two seconds passed and then Kelly launched into 'Flight of the Bumble Bee.' The tempo was dizzying. In two minutes he was halfway through the piece when he transitioned into the old rock version by Bee Bumble and the Stingers. The crowd responded with whistles and cheers. After a minute of that, Kelly stopped again, and started up with his original boogie groove. He sang his new lyrics. It felt great.

Kelly sat at a small table and signed autographs, CD covers, and even a few well-worn album covers. An attractive woman hung back until nearly everyone had left. She came forward and told Kelly how much she enjoyed the concert.

"Are you too tired to get a drink?" she asked.

Kelly was starting to say his regular reply of, "Never too tired to share a drink with a film actress," but he changed his mind.

"I'm beat, and I've got a sore throat. It's gonna be an early night for me," he said. "Thank you so much for your offer."

She was embarrassed and slipped away. Just behind her stood Jack. He was holding hands with his friend.

"This is Carl," said Jack, presenting him to Kelly.

"You were on fire tonight," said Carl.

"Thanks. It was a good one, that's for sure."

"The mikvah, it went well?" asked Jack.

"I think you know the result, Jack. Thanks for the guidance."

"Sure thing, Irish. We expect no less from you when you get back to the Bluebird. And don't forget to ask Steve for a hotel stipend. They give it to people who pack the place, and you packed it."

"I heard that you helped."

"We do what we can," said Jack smiling and giving Carl's hand a gentle tug to get going.

Kelly started packing up his gear on stage and Steve approached him. "Just leave it here, Kelly. You're on tomorrow. It'll be safe. Did you book a room in town?"

"No, not yet. I was gonna to swing by Maison Restaurant and see if my room is vacant."

"You don't know?"

"Know what?"

"They closed. Michael had a heart attack, made it through okay, but it scared him. He and his wife sold the place. It's under renovation. Shut up tight."

Kelly's heart stopped for a few beats at the news. He tried to swallow but couldn't. His throat was suddenly dry and sore. "I had no idea."

"Yeah, it was sudden. He's been a great supporter of road guys like you. I know you two are tight. You should see him while you're in town."

"I will," said Kelly.

"Here's a bit of good news: You packed the place and I'm gonna give you three nights at Breakers Inn down the street. It includes dinners, breakfasts, and laundry service. It's nice. You deserve it. You absolutely slayed 'em tonight. The best I've ever seen you play. I mean it."

Kelly looked up. He'd known Steve for decades and never gotten a compliment like that. Here was a guy who knew music. Kelly studied Steve's face. His long gray hair brought into a tight ponytail, a short goatee, and smiling eyes with honest wrinkles. *A good face.*

"Thanks, Steve. That means a lot coming from you."

"Sure. I'm looking forward to tomorrow when you open for Kit Wells. You should be the headliner, but, well, you know the public. They're fickle."

That reminded Kelly that he wasn't top of the bill for Friday and Saturday. That produced two reactions. He was let down because the next two nights weren't his, and his pulse picked up because he had to write charts for the bass player and drummer.

Kelly helped himself to a microwave burrito and a beer as the crew swept the floors and straightened the chairs. The Freight was like a homecoming to him and he began envisioning what the next two nights would have in store for him. He'd be on stage playing new material with a combo. He hadn't done that for years.

Kelly took one guitar with him and drove to the Breakers Inn. He had some work to do before going to sleep. His head was full of new song ideas. It was a gusher that didn't stop until the sun was turning the black night into a dim blue glow.

Eve was three time zones ahead, making breakfast for her and her mother.

"Tell me about this man you met. The musician," said her mother.

"There's not much to say," replied Eve. "He's a nice guy, but I doubt I'll ever see him again. He's on the road all the time." That was all Eve wanted to share. If she got started she was afraid she wouldn't be able to stop. *It was safer to forget Jacob*, thought Eve.

Chapter Eight

Michael Monapolis and his wife Terra were in the crowd the next night. Michael was the newly retired owner of Maison Restaurant in Oakland where Kelly had planned to stay. Kelly was booked for three nights there the following weekend, which was one reason he was shocked to hear that the place had been sold. Michael approached the stage.

"Hey, Mikey. I hear you had some heart issues. How are you?" asked Kelly.

Michael looked up and smiled sheepishly. He was a shadow of his former self. His hair seemed thinner and grayer, his cheeks were drawn, and some of the sparkle was missing from his dark eyes. Everyone liked Michael. He was a patron of the arts and many musicians were going to miss his restaurant, the gigs, great food, accommodations, and his friendship.

"I'm so sorry I didn't call and tell you. Steve said you were planning to come by and stay. We've been working through a lot. The gig next weekend, well, I'm really sorry, Kelly. I really am."

"You should be, man. I would expect a respectable guy to call me while he's being wheeled into the emergency room.

Hey, doctor, wait a minute, I have to call Kelly to cancel his gig. Yeah, Mikey, you really crapped out on me!"

That made Michael laugh, and his old grin was back. Kelly jumped down from the stage and the two men embraced.

"Terra and I are looking forward to seeing you with a combo." Michael gestured to Terra, who waved from the back of the room. "We haven't seen you play with anyone since the old band days. I remember those times. You sold out the Concord Pavilion!"

"Well that's a great memory. Actually, I was second on the bill for the Northern California Rock Festival. The Jefferson Airplane, I mean the Jefferson Starship, was the band that sold the place out. I like your memory better than mine."

"Yeah, I guess you're right," said Michael, chuckling. "Terra and I would love to have you over for dinner. How about Sunday? You can stay over if you want. There's something I want to tell you. I think you'll be interested."

"That sounds great! What time on Sunday?"

"Come by around 5. We can talk before dinner. I may be a little slow after the heart attack, but my cooking is better than ever. I'm in the kitchen every night."

"Great."

The drummer and bass player took their places and started looking through the song notes. The bad news was they hadn't shown up before the sound check to go over the tunes. The good news was both men had come on stage before the gig started, so they were planning to play the entire set, instead of just doing a few tunes at the end.

Kato Burgess, the bass player, looked at his copies, looked up at Kelly, turned his pages upside down, and made a silly face. Kato was always the joker, and this stunt made Kelly laugh. The charts were three pages of scribbles, not traditional music script. The writing was big with large readable chord symbols and measures indicated with slashes. Kelly had clearly indicated the repeats with bold arrows and he knew Kato was perfectly capable of following them.

"I've never seen these tunes," said Kato, grinning. He had spent four years in the Kelly Jacobs band and he was visibly excited to be on stage with Kelly again. "I hope we're going play some of your old stuff too."

"We can do that," said Kelly, shaking Kato's hand. Kelly walked over to Ben Carter, the drummer. "Hi, I'm Kelly. Thanks for helping me out."

"Man, this is an honor. I love your music," replied Carter. He was a big black man with a short cropped natural and a neatly trimmed beard. He looked more like a jazz player than a folk rock guy. He spun a drumstick around on his left fingertips as he positioned his tom tom with his right. Kelly sensed his talent just by the way he adjusted the drums and set the cymbals.

Kit Wells always attracted the best players, thought Kelly.

Kelly called one of his old tunes to start the set. The guys fell right in behind. The crowd applauded their approval. It was "Carry Me Away," the song that launched the Kelly Jacobs Band into the spotlight. Having experienced players backing him up was something Kelly hadn't done for years. It ignited him, and he went into a ripping solo after the first two verses. There were shouts of encouragement from the audience.

After two original tunes, Kelly put down his guitar and introduced his fellow players. Then he went over to the piano and started playing without even counting off the tune. He was playing a Mozart piece at an accelerated rate. The energy in the room was palpable. People stopped what they were doing and stared at Kelly. After a minute of that, he stopped abruptly, shouted "Song 3!" to the band and counted them into a driving composition.

The form of each tune was familiar, at least at the onset. All pop music is similar in many ways and good players can follow it easily. But Kelly's tunes had interesting and unexpected changes after their beginnings. As was Kelly's songwriting style, he put the hook right up front, often in the first line. That was the simple part. Kelly used head and hand gestures to signal the time and the breaks. The guys were alert and responsive. Then came the tough parts, and Kelly shouted out the place in the form where the changes occurred. Kato was right on, remembering back to a time when Kelly would introduce new material onstage with no warning. Kato hadn't done this kind of playing since he was with Kelly last, over 15 years ago. Kato and Kelly exchanged glances, each grinning from ear to ear.

Ben hung in there and inserted flourishes at every opportunity, as if he'd played the tune a dozen times. They all fed off each other and when the time came for a piano solo, they dropped down and fell into a deep groove. Kelly's solos were taken over a simple three-chord vamp that he'd underlined on the page. They all started out quietly and followed Kelly as he ramped up the volume and the complexity.

The beat was pulsating. People got up and danced in front of their seats. No one was more amazed than Kelly. He hadn't touched a piano in nearly 8 years, until a couple of days before when he'd convinced Steve to leave it on stage. It was all there; his dexterity, the stretch of his left hand to achieve a tenth and the control of the sustain pedal. It was as if he'd never laid off. Like riding a bicycle only louder.

The crowd remained on their feet after he finished the tune. Kelly nodded and smiled at the crowd. He took a look at the clock on the back wall and realized he was almost ten minutes over his time. Getting up from the bench, he walked over to the mic on center stage.

"Thank you. Thank you." Kelly used his hands to motion for the crowd to settle down. When they were quiet, he spoke.

"This has been great for me, because I've been out of circulation for a while. The opportunity to open for the great Kit Wells is big fun. I want to thank Kit for lending me Kato Burgess on bass," Kelly waited for the applause to subside, "and Ben Carter on drums. These guys are great!" More applause. "After a short break to reset the stage, we're in for a big treat. The amazing Kit Wells is coming up here to play the tunes from his latest CD, *Awaken*, which will be for sale at the back table."

Kit Wells walked onto the stage and put his arm around Kelly. He leaned over and spoke into Kelly's ear, "Man, you're gonna be tough to follow. What's gotten into you? I haven't seen you play like that, well, I've never seen you play like that! You're not getting' away with it."

Kit grabbed the mic away from Kelly. "Thank you, Kelly! How about this guy? Does he still have it, or what?" The crowd whistled and clapped. "Well, he's not getting away so soon." Kit turned to Kelly, "Will you play with me for the rest of the night?"

People shouted their approval. The blood in Kelly's veins was pumping hard and fast. After a 15-minute break he took the stage with Kit, Kato, and Carson. There was a set list on the piano and a stack of charts, all arranged in order. Kelly fell in behind Kit and only soloed briefly when called upon. The crowd was enthusiastic, but they didn't react the same way as they had earlier.

On the last song of the evening, Kit asked Kelly to put on a guitar and sing a duet with him. The song was a cover tune from Kit's new CD. It was a blues entitled "Dust My Broom" written by the legendary Robert Johnson. This was a tune the guitarist played with a slide; a glass tube cut from a liquor bottle, placed onto the pinky finger of his left hand. The slide clanked and clattered on the strings and showcased the raw, hard charging delta style blues that was making Kit famous.

Kelly knew the words and he sang a tight harmony part as Kit took control of the tune with his delta style playing. Kelly just played a backup part on guitar and held himself in reserve.

When the time came for solos, Kit was off and running with a series of blistering guitar gymnastics. Everybody was up on their feet again. Carter was hard at work on drums, laying down a funky New Orleans 'second line' rhythm. Then to Kelly's surprise, Kit pointed at Kelly to take a solo.

Kelly turned his guitar up all the way, but it wasn't nearly loud enough. If he tried to solo, it would be buried. He looked around, making sure he had the band's attention, and then signaled for a hard cut by jumping up and bringing his guitar neck down in a slash. Everyone broke hard, including Kit, who was programmed to stop when anyone gave that signal.

While this was going on, Steve had made his way to the soundboard and reached over the shoulder of the engineer to move Kelly's volume slider to the top, way into the red. Kelly hit the first note, a bend on the B string, that started his solo with a cry like a wild cat. It was shockingly loud, but he immediately got it under control and continued to play with his right palm dampening the strings. It was a technique that Dick Dale had pioneered with his wild surf music. Kelly played a series of classical arpeggios at a very fast clip. The effect was hypnotic. After a bit of that, he got into a Latin groove and counted the band back in.

From that moment, Kelly was in control. He led the band through a series of jazz changes that Kato could almost follow on bass. Carter was an accomplished player and he jumped right in. Kit was completely lost and was happy to mute his strings and tap on them with his bottleneck slide.

After 12 bars Kelly set up a simpler Latin progression and Kato and Carter locked in. It was then that the soundman dialed back Kelly's guitar to the right volume and enabled him to take off on a blistering solo. The crowd was keeping time with anything they could find. Keys against bottles, chairs being lifted and dropped, hands clapping, whatever. The groove built up, lasting for longer than any of Kit's previous tunes.

Kelly got the band's attention and tapped his head to signal that they were going to the top of the tune. He jumped up in the air and came down with the standard signal. The band made a hard stop and Kit jumped in with the signature slide guitar part that starts Dust My Broom. It was high voltage.

After two encores, the night ended with Steve turning on the house lights. It was the only way he was able to break the spell and clear the room. Kit sold a load of CDs, but not as many as Kelly, who sold every thing he had, including the old cassette tapes. During the time he was signing CD covers, he felt a hand on his shoulder. He turned, but no one was there. In a few moments, it happened again.

It was Anna, patting him on the back. Encouraging him. Pushing him forward. Setting him on his new path. A warm and calming feeling settled over Kelly and he knew he had her blessing.

Chapter Nine

On Sunday night, Kelly arrived at the Monapolis home at 5PM. The sky was peppered with small high clouds, turning

pink in the winter sky. Kelly checked to see that his shirt was
tucked in. He had bought it earlier in the day at a shop on
Telegraph Avenue in Berkeley. The shop had been one that
Anna liked. Kelly had a wallet full of money from his CD sales
and an additional $400 that Kit Wells had given him. Kit had
also asked Kelly to join him on a tour he was negotiating. Kelly
could feel the gears in his life starting to turn again.

Terra Monapolis greeted Kelly at the door with a hug.
She had her black hair cropped short with purple streaks. Her
eyes were done in a Cleopatra way that young Greek girls did
when they went out dancing in Athens. Terra was at least 50,
and she planned to be youthful forever.

"That was quite a show you put on at the Freight. I was
concerned about Michael. He was dancing!"

Kelly smiled and followed Terra into their expansive
kitchen. Michael hugged Kelly and handed him a glass of
Greek wine.

"Wow, Kelly, that was really a great show!" said
Michael. "You never played like that at our place."

"Well, the restaurant is a different venue than the
Freight."

"Come to think of it, I've *never* seen you play like that.
What's up?"

"Are you in love?" asked Terra.

The question stunned Kelly. *Am I in love?* He had to
pause and think about it. "Yes, I think I am. With a woman I
recently met in Monterey."

"I'm glad to hear it. You were black for a long time," she
said.

"Black?"

"We say *skoteinos*. It means somber, in mourning. From losing Anna." Terra had both her hands on her heart. "She was a princess, that woman. One of a kind. But you're emerging now. I can see it."

"Is it that obvious?" Kelly asked.

Terra reached over to the back of Kelly's head and grabbed a handful of his long hair, like Greek mothers do to their sons. "Of course, it's obvious. Everyone can tell, especially women. It's like you've got a flashing sign on your head. It looks good on you!" she said.

"I admit, I've had a few good things happen to me lately. I feel like I'm beginning a new path. Like Anna gave me her blessing."

"Yes, that's it, of course. We have the same in our culture. It's a gift from the departed," said Terra.

"It can be a challenge too," said Michael. "The departed one encourages the living to try hard, reach for the top, achieve fame in battle or business. It's *agonizomani mechri thanatou*. It translates to *Succeed or Die Trying*. That's what Anna wants you to do. She's giving you a challenge, and she intends to help you, or watch you die trying." Michael was straight faced when he said this.

"Miko! Stop that! You're scaring Kelly," said Terra. She poured more wine into Kelly's glass. "It's just a Greek expression, Kelly. Anna doesn't want any harm to come to you."

Kelly saw Terra and Michael exchange glances and he felt a chill go through him.

Upon Michael's urging, they all moved to the living room and dropped onto the oversized couches. Grabbing big pillows to prop themselves up, they drank their wine in silence.

Emerging from black was just what was happening, thought Kelly. Anna's spirit had something to do with the wonderful nights at the Freight. Kelly was being encouraged to use all his talents to launch a new career. He took chances on stage. That was it. *Succeed or die trying.*

"Kelly, I have something I'd like to tell you," said Michael, breaking the quiet moment. "It's even more appropriate after seeing you play last night."

"Sure, what is it?

"The big networks have been doing various music competition shows, like the Voice, and America's Got Talent. NBC is launching another one using performers from the 1980's and mid 90's. These performers are going to appear in their original costumes, playing their hits. It's called "Where Are They Now?" You could get in there. The first season is just west coast bands. You were a stand out last night. You could win the competition."

"Has the show started yet?" asked Kelly.

"No. I heard about it from my niece. She works in L.A. at a booking agency. She knows that I'm in contact with musicians who were big." Michael looked down sheepishly. "You know what I mean."

"Sure, Mikey, I know. I'm one of those guys. I was big. It was great. Anna and I traveled first class, ate well, spent two months a year in Mexico. I was big. But big doesn't last."

"No, it doesn't. Nothing does. I learned that last month. I was dead for almost five minutes. It changed me. Not just physically. When I sip this wine," Michael lifted the glass and looked through it," My sense of taste is enhanced. It may be my last glass, or I may have 1000 more. I don't know. But I'm savoring every bit of it, and when I get my strength back, I'm going to open another restaurant. I want to die while I'm cooking! Having been big doesn't mean you can't be big again."

"I know. I was big when I was a kid. I played classical piano. Then I faded and became big as a rocker," replied Kelly.

"That's what I'm talking about," said Michael with a big smile. "Some of us are like comets, coming around every decade or two and lighting up the sky."

Kelly, Michael and Terra had eaten many meals together at Maison Restaurant. It was customary for Michael to make a full dinner for his musician friends and eat with them after the customers were gone. This dinner was different. Better in every way.

"You know what I thought when Steve told me you had a heart attack and sold the restaurant?"

"Tell me."

"I thought that we'd never break bread again. That was what hit me. We'd never be able to do this again. But, here we are. You two are such a gift to me." Kelly raised his glass and they drank deeply.

"Tell me about this woman you've met," said Terra.

"Well, she's difficult to describe."

"That's a good thing," replied Terra.

"She lost her husband around the same time I lost Anna. Her name is Eve. She's been coping better than me. She's organized, with a very neat house, clean sheets, healthy foods, and close friends. She's kind. Very kind."

"She sounds nice," said Michael. "Did you have an effect on her, like she affected you?"

"I think I did. I hope so."

"Where is this girl? Bring her here. We want to meet her," demanded Terra with a grin.

"She's gone back east visiting her mother and sisters. I hope to reconnect with her after I make my tour through Portland and Seattle. She's moving, but she'll leave me her new address."

"Don't let her slip away, Kelly. Let me tell you a story," said Terra. "A beautiful girl name Oreaha lived on the Island of Kyros. She had black hair long enough to reach her feet. When she would bathe in the sea, her hair would surround her like a school of fish. One day, when she was floating like that, Cyros, a man with wings, saw her and fell in love. They made love in the sea and the gods were all pleased, except Poseidon. He didn't want a winged man seducing a sea nymph. 'The air is for birds and the ocean is for sea nymphs,' he said.

"Poseidon made the sea angry and the waves rose up, frothy and powerful, to tear the couple apart. Oreaha went deep beneath the waves to take refuge with her mother and sisters. Cyros, the man bird, took flight and circled above the storm

77

until the waves died, but Oreaha did not rise to the surface. He knew she had just gone to visit her family and was sure she'd show up again, but Poseidon wouldn't allow it. To this day, birds scan the sea and often dive down to search for Oreaha."

"That's sad. How could Cyros have held onto Oreaha?" asked Kelly.

Terra didn't answer at once. She sat back and ran her fingers through her hair. "Cyros could have lifted her from the sea and flown away with her, but that didn't happen."

Kelly asked, "Did they ever get together?"

"They did. Cyros sang a song that attracted sea nymphs and when they came to him, he searched their faces to find Oreaha. There were many pretty nymphs, but not the one he wanted so he changed the song so only Oreaha would know that it was Cyros calling for her.

"When Poseidon was sleeping, Oreaha followed the song to the surface and there she met Cyros and they made passionate love. Their children are the flying fish that follow the boats, riding along the crest of their bow wakes."

"That's an interesting story", said Kelly.

Terra leaned forward and kissed Kelly on the cheek. "You may be Cyros. Don't lose track of Oreaha." With that, Terra and Michael rose and went to their bedroom.

Kelly had a lot to think about. He didn't want to lose his connection with Eve, but he had to complete this tour. Michael's comments about Anna's challenge to succeed or die trying were the last words that ran through his mind as he fell asleep.

Chapter Ten

The next morning was overcast and chilly. Kelly awoke to the smell of fresh baked bread. Despite so much wine the previous evening, he felt clear headed. He followed the aroma to the kitchen, where Terra was humming a tune to herself while she pulled out a hot casserole dish from the oven.

"Spanakopita! My favorite!" said Kelly.

"Oh my. We're speaking Greek now, are we?"

"Only what you've taught me, and every word has to do with food. Where's Miko?"

"Don't let him hear you call him that. He likes it when you call him Mikey. You're the only one who calls him that, and I'm the only one that uses Miko, except for his dead mother, who he's been talking with a lot lately."

"Where is he?"

"He's walking around the block. Since the heart attack, he's been walking. He's determined to get strong and open a souvlaki place. You know souvlaki?"

"Yes, of course. There was a great souvlaki place in Syntagma Square in Athens. I ate there many times."

"Where in Syntagma? On the palace side?"

"On the opposite side."

"There were two souvlaki places on that side. When were you there last?"

"About 16 years ago."

"Okay. One place was owned by the Hatzimarkos family. Short fat people with three daughters. The other place was -"

"The Damir family," said Kelly without hesitation.

Terra laughed. "Yes. Turks. But their souvlaki was the best on the square, as much as it pains me to say it. Why were you there and how can you remember them?"

"I performed in Athens several times when I played classical piano. Then a European tour brought the Kelly Jacobs band there, and I ended up staying over for a few weeks. Then again with Anna. Athens is a great place. As far as remembering the Damir family, I have no idea where that came from. My senses seem to be heightened lately. Why don't you move back now the restaurant is sold? Don't most Greeks retire back home?"

"We're not most Greeks. We're more American than Greek now. Our grandchildren are here. They don't even know what spanakopita is."

Just then Michael came through the front door. He was wiping the sweat and mist from his face with a towel. "Kelly! Up early, no?"

"The aroma."

"Yes, it's great!" He gave Terra a pat on her behind and went to the stove to make coffee. "Did you give any thought to the TV show I mentioned?"

"Sure. But I'd really like to play new stuff, not the old material."

"That's the part I didn't tell you. The winner gets to perform new material. But you gotta win first."

"How do I get considered for the show?"

"You go to L.A. and audition."

"That's a long drive."

"Don't drive. Fly from Oakland."

"That's a little pricey. We don't even know if I can get an audition."

Terra smiled. "It's tomorrow, Kelly," she said. "Michael's going with you. He already bought the tickets."

"Really? How did you get it set up so fast? When did you give them my name?"

"When my niece told me about the show," replied Michael. "That was before my heart attack. You're the only one I recommended."

"That was at least a month ago. Why is the audition tomorrow?"

"I called her after we saw you at the Freight. Woke her up. I knew you wouldn't be here long, and I had her push the date up. Are you ready?"

"I guess so, but I don't have a band."

"They won't care about that after they see you perform. A lot of the old bands have broken up, so it's mostly the front men at the auditions."

"You've really thought this out. I won't disappoint you."

Kelly spent the day thinking about what tunes he'd play at the audition. He practiced, not that he needed to. Playing his material was like breathing. But he knew it was important to look enthusiastic, and he hadn't done much of that until the gig at the Freight. He decided on his three most popular songs. He reworked some of the arrangements and made sure he could smile and move around a bit while playing. By 4 PM he was satisfied. The audition was in 24 hours.

Michael and Kelly drove to Oakland airport in silence. For the first time in decades, Kelly was nervous. "A lot is riding on this," said Kelly.

"Not really. It's a done deal. All you have to do is play and sing. It's what you do. They already know who you are. They've looked at old videos, checked around to see that you're not in rehab, and decided to call you in."

"I really appreciate this, Mikey."

"It's not all for you, Kelly. My niece will get a sizeable bonus if you're selected. You have to pay her part of your weekly winnings from each week you stay on the show. She'll also get some booking cash on the other end. But the real reason is, I think your time has come around. That wasn't the case when I gave her your name, but after I saw you Saturday night, I knew you were shining bright again."

Kelly sat in the green room at the TV studio and looked at his watch again. It was past four. He had warmed up and warmed up again. He was getting nervous from warming up. Over preparation can be a bad thing. At 4:30 a young woman holding a clipboard came in.

"Mr. Jacobs, come with me."

He followed her down a hallway into a large dark room. He couldn't see anything except a high stool under a single spotlight. There were two mics set up. One for his voice and one for the guitar. She motioned for him to go in. A voice came over some speakers.

"We're short on time. Show us what you've got, Mr. Kelly."

This doesn't feel good, thought Kelly. *Not good at all.* He couldn't see anyone, the room was like a tomb, and he was nervous. The guy on the mic didn't even know who Kelly Jacobs was. *Mr. Kelly? How old was this guy, 12?* Kelly bristled. He knew that he would be viewed as a has-been. *That's what the show was all about.* But he hadn't envisioned auditioning for a punk that didn't even know his name.

Kelly strapped on his guitar as he walked to center stage. He had his back to the seats. He took a step back and kicked the stool hard. It flew out of sight. Then he got close to the mics, still not looking out to the audience, and started to strum the chords to "My Life." He had to hold back his pent-up energy. He ran through the intro and lifted his gaze towards the faceless twerp seated somewhere out there in the dark.

Warming up in the green room had helped a lot. Kelly jumped an octave for the hook and hit every note. It felt so good that he sang the hook two more times before singing the last verse, doing the refrain three more times and ending the tune.

At the end of the song he let the guitar ring and put his lips right up to the mic and whispered, "How many songs do you need to hear before you decide if I still have it?"

There was no answer. Kelly was engulfed in a wave of heat. He'd screwed up. Kicking the stool was out of character for him and he'd let his irritation get the best of him. He hadn't smiled at all.

This has been a disaster.

"Can you do, *Carry Me Away?*" asked the twerp.

Kelly pulled his face away from the mic and launched into a Bach guitar piece that he'd been using to warm up. It was brisk and in the same key as 'Carry Me Away.' After a minute of that he worked his way into the tune.

"That's fine, Mr. Kelly. You don't have to play the whole thing. If we choose you, you'll have to play it like the recording without that classical stuff. Can you do that?"

Kelly nodded.

"That's it. We'll call you if you're in. Thank you for your time."

Kelly got into the car and closed the door. Michael pulled out of the driveway and onto the street. They drove in silence for what seemed like a long time.

"How'd it go?" asked Michael.

"I have no idea. It felt awful. I played well, but the kid who auditioned me sounded like he was in junior high. He didn't even know who I was. He called me Mr. Kelly."

Michael didn't respond. They got to the airport, turned in the rental car and sat in the waiting lounge. Still, there was no conversation. Kelly was deep in thought. It had been a great ride, but a short one. His crappy camper was waiting for him at Michael's house and then a long drive up to Portland for a three-night gig paying $400 a night. Not a bad fee, but considering the price of gas, it was just another step down to the bone yard.

Back at Michael's house Kelly packed his bag and headed for his camper.

"Don't leave, Kelly. Stay the night. We'll have a nice dinner and drink some wine. Please, stay." Terra was persuasive, but Kelly knew he'd be bad company. It was better not to subject his friends to that.

He kissed and hugged them both. "Thanks. I really appreciate your hospitality and getting this set up for me." With that, Kelly got into the truck and pulled away.

"Kelly!! Wait! Kelly!" Michael was running after the camper waiving his cell phone. "Wait!"

Michael reached the camper and nearly collapsed. It was several long moments before he could speak. "You got it Kelly! My niece called." Michael was struggling to catch his breath. "You're gonna be on the show!"

Chapter Eleven

Eve's visit with her mother and sisters was planned for a week, but she had postponed her return, hoping that a few more days in New York would make her want to move back there. It wasn't working. She was dreading the packing up of the house she and Will had lived in for so many years, and she had no idea where she was going to move. Giving notice at her place in Monterey had been a big mistake. Eve was sitting on the single bed in her old room at her mother's house when her cell phone rang.

"Hey sister, how are you today? How was the class reunion?" asked Maria

"It was fun, but strange."

"How so?"

"Several guys I knew, and hadn't dated, attempted moves on me."

"And that's strange?"

"Yeah, when they're married."

Maria laughed. "That's strange, but not unexpected. What about the guys you did date? Any sparks there?"

"Not at all. The one guy I was looking forward to seeing because I had a crush on him in high school was not looking good. He was the most forward and I spent a lot of the night avoiding him. He cornered me for a slow dance and it seemed to last an hour."

"Too bad Kelly wasn't in your class."

"That thought crossed my mind a hundred times, and not just at the reunion."

"Thinking about him a lot, are you?"

"More than I care to admit. He's unlike all of guys here. Unlike any of the men I've ever met."

"Where is he now?"

"I don't know exactly. He was headed up to Berkeley, Portland, Seattle, and Idaho. He's always on the road. I don't know how I'll ever see him again."

"He made a big impression on you."

"Impression is too small a word. He awakened me, and I'm afraid of that."

"So, you're not moving back to New York?"

"Absolutely not."

"I was hoping you'd come to that conclusion."

"I'm sorry I gave up the house, but the landlord has already made new plans and I need to get my stuff out in a week."

"I'll help. We'll move it all into storage and you can stay here for as long as you like. You'll find a new house, if that's what you want. You can start working again."

"Working? I don't know. It's been a long time. I don't have any connections at the university anymore."

"Yes you do, Dr. Evelyn Benson. Jeron Mattis, the history chair, has an opening. I saw him last night at a party. He'll hire you for next semester to fill a space for someone that's leaving on a sabbatical. It's a done deal."

"Sister, you are too much. I love you."

"Of course you do. Call the airlines right now and book a seat tomorrow on American. There's a flight that leaves at noon. Number 407. I'll meet you at baggage in San Francisco."

"Big thanks, Maria. I'll book the flight right now."

Chapter Twelve

Kelly arrived in Portland the day of his gig. He'd been battered by an angry storm, wrestled with a flat tire, and was told by the duplication place that they couldn't get a batch of CDs to Portland in time for his gig. He gave them the address of the venue in Seattle and resigned himself to the fact that he'd miss out on the sales.

Kelly emerged from the men's locker room at the University of Oregon feeling refreshed by the hot shower.

Fortunately, nobody asked for his I.D. That had happened at Portland City College. It was embarrassing.

The stage at Low Point Tavern was small. It was like putting on a little brother's jacket. He'd played there at least 40 times, and he knew the staff. They always treated him well. His request for a corned beef sandwich was answered with a smile from the pretty waitress, who had hardly noticed him when he'd been there 10 months ago. Maybe there was something to that sign Terra said he was wearing on his head.

By the downbeat at 8 PM the place was packed. The storm had increased, and people were soaked when they came in. The owner came up on stage and tapped the mic.

"It is my pleasure to present to you, direct from Paris...Texas, Mr. Kelly Jacobs!" There was scattered applause, but only the people up front were watching him.

"Nice weather, huh?" asked Kelly as he adjusted the mic. "Let's heat this place up." There was no response.

Kelly started with a quick shuffle blues. This was a tune he usually worked up to in taverns, but stronger measures were needed. He kept the riff going as he got right up on the mic and began talking in a low soft voice.

"I'm not from Texas. I hate that place. I was hit in the forehead by a beer bottle there once, and I wasn't even on stage yet."

That drew some laughs and light applause. This talking intro was something Kelly used to do when Anna and he were on the road together. He couldn't remember the last time he'd done it, but it felt good now.

"My mother was a classical pianist. She taught me most of what I know about music. When I was young, I played the piano. I mean I really played that thing. Bach, Mozart, and Rimski of-course-a-koff. She dragged me all over the world and forced me to stay in five star hotels, perform in palaces, and extend my baby finger when I drank wine from crystal glasses. I gave all that up to play guitar in places like this.

"Now I'm back here in Portland, the city of roses. And if you don't stuff that tip jar, I'm gonna starve to death!"

Kelly launched into Crossroads by Robert Johnson. He sang low. It was at the very bottom of his range, but he was hitting all the notes. He ended the first verse and looked up.

"Someone give me a knife. I need a knife!"

A woman leaned forward and handed Kelly a knife with mayo smeared on it.

"A clean knife!" He said. She wiped it off and handed it back to him. He slid it along the strings from the lowest position to the octave on the 12th fret. It made a wailing sound. He began his story with slow talking low tones.

"A long time ago, in the Mississippi Delta, there was a black man named Robert Johnson. He was poor, and he was an okay guitar player. Back in those days, only wealthy people could afford good instruments, and Robert Johnson's guitar was bad. Not just bad, but awful. He couldn't even play a chord on it because the strings were so high and the neck was so warped. So, he played the guitar with a bottle neck. I would have asked for that, but I told you about my Texas experience already."

Kelly had the attention of everyone by now. He slid the knife along the strings and set up a solid groove. Along with his foot stomping, the house had what was needed to come alive.

"Robert Johnson had limited success as a musician, but that didn't stop him. He learned from older players, practiced constantly, and made some improvements. But that wasn't enough, so he left town in search of... well... something. And he found it."

Kelly sang the verse again. "I went down to the crossroads..." Then he went back to his talking voice.

"Nobody knows the truth about where the crossroads are, or who Robert met down there, but when he returned to town, he was a brilliant performer. He played the best juke joints, got married at least three times to two different women, and rose to the top of his profession.

"It was rumored he made a deal with the devil. He sold his soul in exchange for becoming the best blues man ever. It worked. But every debt has its due date, and one night, when Robert was getting close to another man's wife, he died. It wasn't a gunshot, or a knife, it was poison whisky."

Kelly sang the last two verses and ended the song. Loud applause and cheering erupted at once. It grew louder and then tapered off. Kelly kept the momentum throughout the set. By the end of the night there was over $300 in his tip jar.

Seattle was better than Portland. Kelly worked up some more stories and his audience grew each night. He was featured on the radio and the place where he played held him over for two more weeks. Kit Wells rolled into town and asked Kelly to perform with him at the Seattle Theater. It was a concert venue with a grand piano. Kelly opened the show and Kit came on to sing with Kelly's piano accompaniment. Just like in Berkeley, the night was fabulous.

Everything was coming together and then the accident happened.

A guy in a pickup truck ran a light and hit Kelly's camper broadside. There were no broken bones, but Kelly's left arm was in a sling and he had 6 stitches on his cheek. The side of his face was black and blue. Kelly couldn't even lift a glass with his damaged hand, and the other one was always in pain. The big foam collar around his neck was especially charming.

Kit finished the Seattle portion of his tour without Kelly and went on to Vancouver. Kelly stayed in a cheap hotel to recover. He had no camper to carry him anywhere else.

"Is this all you need from there? You know you won't be able to come back. We're gonna crush this thing. It's not drivable." The man at the junkyard was sympathetic. He was about Kelly's age but rougher around the edges. Greasy hands, a soiled baseball cap and a scruffy gray beard that could be housing cockroaches.

Kelly held a bag of clothes in one hand, and Eve's Wedgewood coffee grinder in the other. He'd found a metal lipstick tube from Anna under the passenger seat, and he put that into his pocket. He had a cane, but it was impossible to use with both hands full, so he let it fall to the ground. "Yeah, that's it," replied Kelly.

While Kelly was walking away the guy said, "Hey, you're the singer, aren't you? I saw your picture on the news. People are looking for you."

"Who's looking for me?"

"I think it's some people in L.A. Television people. Something about a song contest."

"Really?"

"Yeah, it was on TV last night. You should call the station. You can use the phone in my office."

It was painful for Kelly to dial the greasy ancient phone. Every bone in his arm complained when he moved. "This is Kelly Jacobs. I hear you did a bit about me on the news. Someone is looking for me?"

"Mr. Jacobs, please hold, I'll contact the news desk." There was a long pause and a woman came on the phone.

"Kelly Jacobs? The performer?"

"Yes, that's me."

"Great. This is great! There's a TV producer looking for you. You've become the center of a pretty big human-interest story. You're supposed to appear on an upcoming show, right?"

"Yes."

"Well, that's an NBC show. We're an NBC affiliate. They're using your disappearance to hype the show. It's a big story."

"I didn't disappear."

"Sure, you did. Where are you? We'll send a car to get you."

Kelly

Kelly did a TV interview that afternoon. He wanted to take off his foam collar, brush his hair and shave, but the director didn't want Kelly to look pretty. The make up artist added more dark stuff to his face to make him look worse.

The questions were leading ones, and they came quickly, not giving Kelly time to form thoughtful answers.

What caused you to drop out of society? What's it like living as a homeless person? Were you hooked on drugs? Do you recall any of the details about your car crash?

Kelly felt as though he was alert and honest with the questions, but when he viewed the interview on TV that night, he appeared to be caught off guard and confused. It was a bad showing for him, but a good one for NBC. The station set up a fund to 'Help Kelly Jacobs Play Music Again.' In the next week $15,000 came in along with a truck and a camper. The vehicle was almost new. It was donated by a local car dealership. Kelly had to go there and be photographed accepting the keys. A cell phone company gave him a new phone with a full year of fees paid upfront. A beauty parlor did a before and after makeover and the photos went viral.

"I don't know what's happening, Terra. I thought I was doing well. Playing better. Moving forward. Now I'm a charity case." Kelly tried to control his voice, but he ended up crying. He pulled the phone away from his ear and wiped his eyes with his sleeve.

"Kelly, are you there? Kelly?"

"Yeah, Terra, I'm here."

93

A Beggar's Tune

"You aren't the one that's doing this. It's Anna. She's making things happen. We love you. Anna loves you. What's going on now is beyond friendly assistance and coincidence. You see that, don't you?"

"I don't believe in ghosts, or at least I didn't."

"Not ghosts, spirits. Helpful spirits. Maybe it's your parents too. Don't discourage or disappoint them. You've got momentum now and it won't last forever. Point yourself at a goal and start pedaling. This is your time."

Kelly was settling down now. Terra's advice was soothing. His cheap hotel room was looking more like a temporary stop over than the bone yard he imagined it to be just a few days ago.

"Thanks, Terra. You make me feel better."

"Good. And what about that woman you told us about. Have you contacted her?"

"No. I wanted to, but things were so busy. I never got her phone number. I didn't even own a phone. I've sent a few cards, but I have no address to receive replies."

"Use our address. This is your home now," said Terra.

"What's on your schedule next?" It was Michael on the extension.

"Hi, Mikey. I'm booked in Vancouver next Friday, but I can't play yet. My hand is still bandaged, and I can't even lift my arm to grab the fret board. I'm gonna cancel. After that I'm in Denver at a crappy tavern for a few days, a music festival in Vail, and another bunch of dates in Idaho. Kit asked me to join his tour after Idaho. I'll meet him in Missoula, Montana. I

94

should be okay by then. He has 20 cities to go. That will keep me busy until late May."

"My niece says you'll be introduced on the first episode of the show in June. The taping will be on May 25th. You've got to be in L.A. for that. You'll need to be dressed like you were in your band days. Do you still have any of that stuff?"

"No. It's long gone. Since the accident I'm down to one bag of clothes."

"No problem." It was Terra. "I'll get a few outfits for you from local thrift shops. You can stay here for a few days and rest before the show."

"What about money and a car? You have that worked out?" Michael asked.

"I've got that under control. And I have a cell phone now. I'll give you the number."

"We can see the number in caller I.D." said Terra.

"Oh yeah, silly me. Of course, caller I.D," but he had no idea what that was.

"Okay. Let's stay in touch. We want to hear from you every couple of days. Please," said Michael.

"Of course. Thank you so much. I love you both."

Kelly settled the bill at the hotel desk. The girl behind the counter had tattoos along her arms and up her neck. The double nose rings were a nice touch, and really helped compliment her black leather bra and pajama bottoms.

"Hey, do you know how to see caller I.D. and set up a voice box?" asked Kelly.

She laughed. "You mean voice mail?"

"Yeah, voice mail."

"Sure, I can help you with that."

By the time Kelly pulled up to the entrance with his new camper she had his phone set up and a sheet of paper with handwritten instructions for him. There were bullet points like Google, Mapquest, and a few other sites including her personal Facebook page. Everything was accessible through speed dial. She explained it all to Kelly like he was 90 years old.

"I'm Marie. Where you goin' after you leave here? My friend is having a party. She's turning 25. You can come with me and stay over at my place. You'll be a big hit there. People have seen you on the news."

"Wow, that's a great offer, but I've gotta hit the road. Thanks for your help."

"Can I take a picture with you?"

"Of course."

She came around the desk and positioned Kelly next to an aquarium with plastic fish. The pump was running, but the fish were just floating on the surface. Kelly really hadn't bothered to look at the lobby until now. The decorations were quirky. A lime green couch with orange pillows, eight old TVs on shelves against the wall, a big stuffed llama, and some cowboy gear scattered around. Draped over a chair was a coat that seemed familiar to Kelly.

Kelly stood next to Marie with his arm over her shoulder while she took some selfies. "I sent the last shot to you. It was the best. It's going out on Facebook. I have over 5,000 friends."

Kelly looked impressed, but didn't know what Facebook meant.

"Hey Marie, what's the story with that leather jacket"?

"A guy left it here about a year ago. It's a real flight jacket from WWII. I've seen ones just like it in movies. Pretty cool, huh?"

Kelly inspected it. It was similar to the one he owned when he was touring with the band. The element that captured his attention was the canvass identification label sewn just above the right front pocket. *Kelly, Airman 1st Class.* That should have been spooky, but it wasn't. *Why wasn't it odd,* Kelly asked himself. It was another intervention and he didn't want to jinx it by thinking too hard.

"Wanna sell it? I used to have one, but it's gone now."

"I guess. It's good retro. I could get $175 for it at a store."

"How about $125? I really like it."

"$150 and it's yours."

Kelly emerged from the Vagabond Hotel in Seattle wearing the worn leather flight jacket. It felt comfortable, like an article of armor made especially for him. The sky was starting to clear and the roads would be safe all the way to Monterey. It wasn't on the way to Denver, but he had his heart set on seeing Eve.

Chapter Thirteen

Kelly rolled into town at 2:15 AM. He drove straight to Eve's house. It looked dark and different. There were sheets covering the windows, and the wooden porch had been replaced with cement. Buckets of paint and pieces of wallboard were stacked on the side of the property. The tree in the front yard had been removed. Kelly thought he was on the wrong street and checked the house number, but it was correct. Right address, too late.

He parked his camper in the driveway and slept there until dawn. Then he sat on the cold cement porch and asked passersby if they knew where the woman who lived here had gone. By 11 AM he decided to knock on doors. Neighbors were remote and guarded. A police cruiser pulled alongside Kelly as he walked to the last house on the block.

"Hey buddy, what'cha doin?" said a cop, leaning out the car window.

Kelly came over to the policeman. "I'm trying to find out where Eve went. She used to live in that house. Lived there for decades. Now she's gone."

"Why do you want to find her?"

"Because I love her, and I want to marry her. Nothing more."

The cop smiled. "Why didn't she tell you where she went?"

"She left me her forwarding address in the hole in that tree. I mean the tree that used to be there." Kelly pointed at the freshly cut stump.

"Got an I.D?" the cop asked.

Kelly pulled his wallet out and the cop viewed it with interest. It was stuffed with money from the funds raised in Seattle. Kelly handed over his driver's license and stood still as the cop ran his name and info. The cop's partner leaned over to look at Kelly. Then the policemen exchanged a few words.

"You're the singer. The guy that disappeared and was found in Seattle. Right?"

"I didn't disappear. I just became unfamous and then got broadsided by a driver who ran a stop sign. There's a TV show that hyped up the story. I didn't disappear."

"That checks out," said the other cop as he paged through displays on the computer mounted on the dashboard.

"Okay, you're good. Stop stalking this woman. Don't make us sorry we let you go." The cop handed Kelly's license back to him and drove away.

Kelly returned to Eve's old house and sat on the porch. The place had nothing for him. No lingering cooking smells or aroma of Eve. Nothing.

What now?

He made a mental list of the most important things he wanted to accomplish. Finding Eve was at the top, but there were survival tasks that took precedent. Performances, driving, more performances. Kelly headed for the Bluebird Café. He had questions and Jack would have answers.

"She's gone. The tree she left her forwarding address in has been cut down."

"Irish, you're not making any sense. She carved her address on a tree?" Jack was shaking his head.

As the two men sat in the empty tavern over coffee, Kelly recounted the story to Jack, who listened and nodded.

"Romantic, but not practical. What's her last name? Maybe she has a trail we can find on the internet."

Kelly's face was blank.

"Her name, Irish. What's her last name?"

"I never asked. I never do. That leads to questions about me, my name, my past, you know. I never asked."

"Good god, man. You told her your real name and your history. You slept with her for two weeks. You ate her home cooked meals, and you never asked her last name?"

"No."

"This makes things difficult. Carl is good with internet stuff, but he's not a magician. Maybe he can find out the owners of the house and get a lead. Meanwhile, you need to work on your bird song."

"Bird song?"

"Yeah, bird song. Male birds have a certain song they use to attract a mate. The better the song, the nicer the mate. Lions roar, fish blow bubbles, dogs howl; it's all out there. Where have you been?"

"Living as a human."

"Right," replied Jack. "You used a song to attract Anna, right?"

Kelly thought about that. "Yeah, I wrote a song about her and she loved it."

"Now you need to write a song that will attract Eve."

"Like Cyros singing to Oreaha."

"That's the birdman and the mermaid, right?" asked Jack.

100

"Yeah, the Greek myth."

"It's not Greek. It's Romanian. They just changed the names. It's Romanian." Jack glared at Kelly.

"Yeah. Great story. So, I write a new song?"

"Not just any new song." Jack leaned forward, getting close to Kelly to command his full attention. "Just a good song will attract lots of women. You need to write a song that will attract one specific woman: Eve. Of course lots of birds will come to that song, but if the song is right, and it makes Eve relive your best time together, she'll find you. That's nature."

Kelly swirled the coffee in his mug. It was mostly grounds now, and he set it down.

Jack took the mug, turned it over, and slammed it onto the table. The sound was loud and sharp. Then he carefully lifted the mug and examined the shape left behind by the sludge.

"What are you doing?" asked Kelly.

"Just checking something. Things look good. You're gonna meet some allies. Be open to opportunities. Lean forward in everything you do, Yacob."

"That's exactly what my grandfather used to tell me! How do you know these things?"

"I can't reveal my sources, except for the one you just figured out. Just do as I say."

"Thanks Jack, you're a guiding light."

"We do what we can, Irish."

Kelly drove east across the Sierra Nevada mountains toward Denver with the Wedgewood coffee grinder on the seat next to him. The new truck and camper was a luxury he wouldn't have been comfortable with a few months ago. Now it felt like home. At a rest stop near Reno, Kelly picked through his old clothes and decided not to keep anything except a recently purchased pair of jeans, the new shirt he'd bought in Berkeley, and the flight jacket. He gave the rest of the stuff, and a hundred dollars, to a couple of guys living in a car.

Dirty snow formed high berms on the sides of the road. The sky was a changing mix of big thunderheads, solid gray, and patches of expanding and contracting blue. Kelly ran though a bunch of possible lyrics for a song that would attract Eve. They all sounded trite. How could he write a song that would bypass his standard method of music construction?

Kelly's normal approach had worked well in the past, but it was an obstacle now. He needed to stop thinking about chord progressions and poetic cadences. The flashes of creativity that fueled his most popular material had to be ignored and stripped away to expose bare ground. Only then could he plant a new seed and nurture it. Deep inside his gut he knew it wouldn't be easy, but it was possible. It would just take time, and maybe some help. Help from the one person he knew was guiding his steps: Anna.

Chapter Fourteen

Kelly reached the outskirts of Denver but couldn't stay awake to drive any further. It was 6 PM and the weather was clear and windy. The gusts blew hard, forcing truck drivers to pull off the road. Kelly's normal low-end motels were all full. He pulled into a Travel Lodge and cradled the coffee grinder against his chest as he pushed the lobby doors open.

"What's the cheapest room you have left?" he asked the desk clerk. The guy was a tall skinny bald man. He ran the fingers of one hand over the polished surface of his head as he punched keys with the other.

"You a veteran?"

"Yes, I am."

"Got your service card or a copy of your discharge papers?"

"No."

"Then you're not a veteran. What about a teacher?"

"No."

"How about handicapped?"

"Just mentally. I'm a has-been musician looking for the woman I just met, fell in love with, and can't find."

"We have a room. It's close to the road, but there's not much traffic with this windstorm. It will be quiet for now. We can give you another one when things open up. With your special discount, it'll be $44 including tax."

"I'll take it."

Kelly went straight into the room, set the Wedgwood down, stripped naked and crawled into bed. He was asleep in five minutes.

When he awoke it was 5 AM. He'd slept for almost 11 hours. He looked around the room. He'd forgotten to bring his instruments in with him. A charge of anxiety raced through him. Slipping into his jeans, he went to the parking lot bare-chested

103

and retrieved his two guitars. He was still walking with a limp and the cold made things worse. The wind was strong, and it was about 35 degrees. He rushed back inside and took a hot shower. He was angry at himself for leaving his instruments in the camper.

The venue for Kelly's first gig in Denver, from what he could remember about it, was a dive. The Sub Par Bar. If it wasn't for the owner, who Kelly liked, he would have cancelled. He showed up about 90 minutes before the downbeat for the free dinner. The place had a new look and the food smelled great.

The waiter came by and asked Kelly if he was ready to order. "Where's Chuck?" asked Kelly.

"Dead."

"No, really, where's Chuck?"

"I'm not kidding. He died and left the place in debt. None of us had been paid for six weeks. That was his way of solving things. I wasn't a fan."

"Wow. I was booked to play here for three days this week."

"You Kelly Jacobs?"

"Yeah, that's me."

"You're still booked, but the pay schedule has changed."

"How?"

"You get $200 a night like before and 5% of the bar. And we charge admission now. It's only two bucks, but you get it all. You okay with that?"

"Sure. What about dinner? Has that changed?"

"Totally new menu."

"I mean, do I get a free dinner?"

"I know what you mean. I'm just messin' with you. Yeah you get a free dinner and one drink per set. We settle at the end of each night. You may have to take part of your pay in quarters when we empty the pool tables."

"That wouldn't be the first time. You mind if I ask you how this place stayed open after Chuck died? It was in debt, so how does that work?"

There was a complete change of attitude from the waiter. He stood up straight and was suddenly engaged with Kelly.

"It was an employee buyout. I own a third, Julie at the bar owns a third, and Juanita and her husband Enrique own the other third. The creditors gave us a chance to make things right over time and we took it. I did all the remodeling."

Kelly looked around. The place was a lot cleaner and the dusty fans were gone. "I'm impressed. Good for you. What's your name?"

"I'm James. I know you're Kelly. I saw your story on the news."

"All the way out here?"

"Actually, on the internet. I did a search for you when I saw your name on the calendar. We cancelled the deadbeats. There were a lot of those. Can I ask you a question?"

"Sure."

"How does a well-known rock star end up on the skids? They said in the story that you were never into drugs or other stuff. You just dropped out."

Kelly didn't want to go there, but this guy had warmed up to him and honored the gig. "My wife died. It killed us both. Her quick and me slow. I hope you never have that happen to you."

"Wow, man. That's bad. But you look good now, except the side of your face is bluish green. The accident, right? You're gonna be on TV! That's good, right?"

"That's real good. Speakin' of good, what's good?" Kelly pointed to the menu.

The place was more than half-full by the time Kelly took the stage. He started with a ballad and got a lukewarm applause. His right hand was working okay, but his left wasn't doing what he wanted it to. He was adjusting a string to kill time when someone yelled, "Make Me a King!"

"Who said that?" asked Kelly while he shaded his eyes and looked over the faces.

A big guy with one leg came forward on crutches. "Me," he announced.

"Hey, Mondo!" yelled Kelly. He got off his high chair and went to the end of the stage to bend down and shake hands. "Long time no see. How's Grace?"

"She's good. She's waving at you. See her, she's over there."

Kelly squinted and saw her at the back. He waved and took his place back on the stage.

"Sorry for the break, but I wanted to say hello to an old friend, Armando Diaz. It's great to see you, man! Mondo was

106

the road manager for the Kelly Jacobs Band for eight years. Eight, right? A damn good musician too!"

"It felt like a year! It was fun!" replied Armando.

"Yeah, it went by fast. So, this song he requested, Make Me a King, was never recorded. I don't think it ever got finished. I doubt I can remember the words. It was written for Mondo's kid, Bernard."

"I remember the words!" shouted Armando.

"Okay then, come up and sing it with me!"

Apparently, Armando was well known at the Sub Par Bar because he got a big applause. Numerous people hoisted him onto the stage. He positioned himself on Kelly's stool and adjusted the mic. Kelly gave his guitar to Armando and took his electric off the stand and plugged it in. James brought another mic on stage for Kelly and they started the song.

Armando strummed an intro and began the vocal. Kelly gave him free reign. His sweet baritone voice brought back memories of the years on the road. Good memories of good years. Mondo stayed for the full first set, singing and playing Kelly's old tunes flawlessly. The crowd was disappointed when the break came, but the place didn't empty out. The tip jar had at least $100 in it. Kelly was glad to get off the stage. His arm, hand, and shoulder ached badly. He wouldn't have done well without Armando's help. Kelly sat down with Armando and Grace.

"How have you been, Kelly?" asked Grace. "We heard about Anna. So sad. A wonderful lady."

"Yes, one of a kind. I'm just getting past it. It's been eight years. Things are good now. I'm writing again and I'm playing piano after a long layoff."

"You were good once. I mean concert good. Tell her Kelly." Armando motioned for him to explain to Grace.

"Sure, I was good. On tour playing classical music. It was a long time ago. How do you know that, Mondo? I don't think I ever said anything about it to you."

"It's on the internet. Just Google your name. You have a Wikipedia page. It shows you getting a big award in Moscow. You're a big shot."

Grace pulled out her phone and ran Kelly's name on Google. It came up as Kelly Jacobs AKA Jacob (Yacob) Kelayoff. There he was, accepting the gold medal in Moscow. There were other photos, including a recent shot of him playing at the Bluebird Café in Monterey. *This was done by Carl, Jack's friend. Who else would do this?* He could see the back of Eve's head in the shot. It took his breath away.

"You okay, Kelly?" asked Grace.

"Sure, I'm fine. I just see someone in the photo. A woman I met there at the gig. That's her, right there." Kelly pointed her head out in the photo. Just touching her image was electric.

"Someone special?" asked Armando.

"Very special."

"Would you like to stay at our house? We have a room. Bernardo went away to college," said Grace. "Having you stay over would be fun."

108

"I don't want to impose."

"You could stay a year and it wouldn't be an imposition. It's settled. I'll leave a little early and you can drive Mondo home in your car. Is that okay?"

"Yes, Grace. That'd be wonderful," said Kelly.

After the gig Kelly loaded up his gear and helped Armando into the truck. Kelly slid into the driver's side and put the Wedgewood on the seat between them.

"What's that?" asked Armando. "It looks like a coffee grinder."

"That's what it is. The woman in the photo gave it to me about a month ago. It never leaves my sight. It's my most valuable possession."

"I guess she had a good grind."

Kelly didn't laugh.

"Sorry, that was crude," said Armando.

"No worries," said Kelly. "She's special and I plan to reconnect with her when I find her. We lost touch. She moved and I don't have her new contact info." Kelly told him the whole story. It felt good to tell private stuff to an old friend.

"You'll find her, Kelly. Things like that happen for a reason. You'll find her."

"How are you, Mondo? How's the leg? You're not wearing the prosthetic. Why?"

"The cancer is back. Goin' in for another operation in a month. I've told Grace the doctors are confident, but they've told me they're not sure. Don't mention that to Grace, okay?"

Kelly nodded. They drove in silence for a while.

"You know, Mondo, the band was at our best with you. You were much more than a road manager. You did great sound, added a lot of positive energy, and were a lot of fun on stage. We all missed you so much when you left. I'm sorry we lost contact."

"Me too. I wanted to call you when I heard about Anna, but I didn't know how to reach you."

"It's okay, no one could have tracked me down. I managed to fulfill my dates for a few months, but then I cut myself off from the world. Without Anna, I'd lost the drive to write tunes and keep a band together. It was a downward spiral. You've heard about people that bottom out and bounce back, but I just settled in a low spot. It wasn't the end, because I never was into drugs or drinking. It was a soft landing in purgatory."

At the house, Kelly helped Armando out of the truck.

"Can I carry a guitar?" asked Armando. "Just for old time's sake?"

Kelly gave him the acoustic and watched him make his way to the front door with some difficulty.

The two men stayed up late. Some of the talk was about the old days, but mostly it was about Armando's future.

"I'm building a cabin with Bernardo up in the Rockies," said Armando proudly. "He's a good worker. We'll use it for getaways. I can't ski anymore, but he can. I can still fish, and there are some good streams up there."

"It's great that you stay active, man."

"I have to. None of us know how long we have. Next summer, Grace and I are doing a road trip on Route 66. If I don't

110

do this stuff now, and my operation fails, I'll be sad. Worse than sad. Now's the time to do what we love."

Kelly listened, but didn't talk much. Here was a guy with issues, but he faced forward and leaned into life with gusto.

"What about you, Kelly? Have you recalibrated?"

"Yeah, I think I have. It happened pretty quick. Eve seems to have lifted a cloud off me."

"You gotta stay with her. A good relationship makes everything better. I'm lucky."

"You are," said Kelly. "You have Bernardo and Grace."

Armando replied, "You have a lot Kelly. A lot. You're healthy, you've got great chops, and your voice is top notch. Plus, you've got this woman! Who could ask for more? You need to move up again. Quit playing little roadhouse gigs. The time is right for you."

As they said good night, Kelly thanked Armando for his friendship and inspiration.

Kelly lay on his back, unable to sleep. His hands and arm throbbed. He reviewed the events of the past few weeks. It had been a whirlwind, all of it propelling him towards a point beyond the horizon. He wished he had a clear vision of what awaited him.

He could move on in the competition, or he could get cut. What would he do if he got cut? Failure was not an option. Cyros and Oreaha kept on track and worked around Poseidon to eventually join in love. It was because of the song.

The song he hadn't written yet.

Kelly tried to envision how the contest would go, but he didn't know who he'd compete against, so constructing an accurate vision wasn't possible.

Every step, every strategy, every muscle should be focused on getting in front of millions of people and singing his birdsong to Eve, so she could emerge from the ocean depths and come to him.

At this time of night, he would normally think about Anna, and he did just that. He didn't want to lose his connection with Anna. Only after some time did he journey back in time and lay with Eve.

Chapter Fifteen

Eve settled into Maria's house and started her class at the university. The work kept her mind occupied during the day, and dinners with Maria were engaging, but laying alone in bed was difficult. She tried to think of Will before falling asleep, but memories of Kelly always crowded everything out. When he appeared in her mind, she always addressed him as Jacob. In conversations with Maria, Eve referred to him as Kelly. Jacob was a secret name that she kept to herself.

Kelly's stay in Denver at Armando's place was good. The next two nights at the Sub Par Bar were profitable and the following week his gigs were within driving distance from Denver.

He was relieved not to sleep in the camper and search for a hot shower. On the third week, he drove to Idaho on icy roads with several near misses. He had known this would be tough going in the winter, but he had to keep working.

Kelly felt his pain fading and most of the discoloration on his face was gone. About 85% of his guitar chops were back, and when there was a piano, he found he could play with no pain at all.

The gigs were similar to the Sub Par Bar, but Kelly had a new mojo and the tip jar was showing results. He'd already sold through the shipment of CDs he'd had made in Seattle and had ordered more.

His rendezvous point with Kit Wells was in Missoula, Montana. Kelly arrived four days early and called Gene Barton, a good soundman who had retired there.

"Hey Gene, this is Kelly Jacobs. How are you?"

"Kelly, my man! Good to hear your voice! Where are you?"

"I'm in Missoula. I'll be connecting with Kit Wells and touring with him for a while."

"Great! I'm doing the sound for Kit here and in Helena."

"I thought you were retired."

"Well, the wife left and the cat died. Didn't have anything to do, so I got dragged back. It feels good."

"I'm lookin' forward to working with you. Hey, I've got a question."

"Shoot."

"I've got some new material. Do you know anyone with a home studio with a piano that could cut a simple CD and duplicate 100 for me? I'd like to sell them at my gigs. My old stuff is old."

"You're joking, right? You know I have a studio with a Steinway."

"I didn't know that. That's great!"

"When do you want to start?"

"Right now."

"I'll put on a pot of coffee and warm the place up. I'm at 206 Washington Street. It's a warehouse. I'm on the third floor. Press the buzzer and I'll open the door. Take the freight elevator up. I'll be here."

Gene looked the same, only wrinkled. His pale gray eyes still sparkled, and his unruly head of hair was pulled back into a squirrel's tail as always. Tall and rangy, with unnaturally long fingers. He had a great touch with a soundboard.

After the obligatory hugs, the two men got right to work. Coffee, pizza, and more coffee. Most of the tunes were done in two or three takes. Kelly always worked fast in the studio, and by 5 AM they had completed 10 new cuts. 60 minutes of new music.

"Wow, Kelly, we did this in one session, and it sounds clean! You've been woodshedding. You have chops on the piano! Your voice sounds strong. Do you want to stay over and hit it again tomorrow?"

"That would be great. I'd like to add some guitar fills and harmony vocals."

"I'm down for that. You can sleep in the room in the back. It's not the Hilton, but it's warm. You got a sleeping bag?"

"Sure. I'll bring it up."

It was that simple. The switch had been turned on and Kelly was producing music again. Things were going his way, and he knew it wasn't just luck. He felt Anna's presence.

That night in the few minutes before he fell asleep he sang "Visions of Anna" to himself over and over again. He hoped she could hear him. He planned to record that song the next day for the first time. It was his torch song to Anna and it had been the song that had impressed Eve. She had told him so.

Kelly hoped that recording Visions of Anna would help him move on and allow him to begin work on the song that would bring Eve to him.

The next day was productive. Kelly completed a good version of "Visions of Anna" on the first take.

"I'll start at the head and you can do some harmony on the refrain," Gene said through Kelly's headset.

"Nope. It's a one take song," said Kelly into the mic. "I wanna keep this one honest. It's fine the way it is. Let's go back to the piano tunes and I'll lay down some guitar work."

"You got it. I wish more guys were this easy to work with," said Gene from the control room.

Each version of Kelly's new tunes evolved through the three or four takes that were done. There was a new force that was emanating through Kelly's fingers into his instruments. A tingling of sorts. After realizing that the first takes were just as good as later ones, Kelly started to worry that he was letting his creative power escape by playing too much. This thought had

115

never crossed his mind before, but it made him anxious now. *What if the flow of creativity was limited? What if Anna only had so much she could give?*

Kelly and Gene worked all day, with Kelly insisting they move through the song list with no more than two takes. They finished the last tune at 6 PM.

"Let me take you out to dinner," said Kelly, pulling off the headphones and putting his guitar on a stand in the corner of the sound room. Kelly straightened his back and felt it crack in a couple of places. He was tired and stiff. His forearm ached from playing so long. All of these pains were familiar, and not from the accident. He'd felt like this many times in the old days and it was satisfying.

Chapter Sixteen

"And it didn't hurt you when Katie left?" asked Kelly, taking another gulp from his long necked-beer. They were sitting at a small table in the back corner of Gene's favorite restaurant, a Thai place in the old section of town.

"I thought it would. I expected to fall apart in a couple of days, but nothing happened. Nada. Zip. My wife leaves me for another guy and I don't even react. I got a dog, started taking long walks at sunrise, cut way back on my drinking, and slept like a baby. It's been two years, Kelly. Two years since I've seen Katie. I haven't spoken with her for," Gene rubbed his forehead and thought about it, "at least six months. The last time we talked, it was tough. She asked to come back and I was firm about saying no. It wasn't revenge. I just don't want to go back there. I'm on a new path. The divorce was final last week. Am I strange, being so unfeeling?"

"I don't think so. We're on a journey. It sounds trite, and we've all heard the B.S. about that before, but it gets repeated often because it's true.

"I fell down a deep hole after Anna died. For eight years I was numb. Then I met this woman, Eve, and she flipped a switch in my brain. The time came for me to emerge, in fact I was way overdue, and she was the catalyst. Totally unexpected."

"My story is a lot less painful," said Gene. "I didn't fall down a hole, I was already there and didn't know it. A guy from Katie's past looked her up after his wife died, and she went for his proposition. Simple as that. Sure it stung, but not as much as you'd expect.

"I moved out, rented the space in the warehouse, and spent all my cash on recording equipment and the Steinway. I didn't have a single prospect. No one recorded a note in the place for two months. I got up every morning, took the dog for a long walk, and came back to spend the day tweaking the mics, playing with the soundboard, dialing the place in. I placed an ad on the corkboard in the music department at the college, and I got a few decent players to hire me for some demos. That's when things picked up."

Kelly liked Gene. He was animated, talking with his hands while he chewed his food, reaching down to pet his dog under the table, joking about himself. He was a good friend that Kelly didn't know he missed until they met up again.

With a new crop of tunes in the bag, Kelly ordered 100 copies from Gene. They were done in time for Kelly's first night with Kit Wells in Missoula. The opening night wasn't packed, but word spread quickly and the rest of the nights in Montana were sold out. Kelly continued his big presence on stage, with Kit's encouragement. In the next ten days Kelly sold his 100 CDs and 100 more. Before leaving the state, he ordered 500 from Gene. This last batch had a photo of Kelly on the cover and the song list printed on the back. Kelly used the same picture of him that Eve had seen in the Good Times newspaper.

Kelly spent most of his free time trying to write what Jack had called the bird song. There was a good one called "All About Eve" on his new CD, but it didn't have the heartfelt compassion that was required to make her relive their time together. That essence eluded him. It was something that Anna couldn't help him do.

Chapter Seventeen

Kit and Kelly continued the 20-city tour. They did radio interviews, duo appearances on local cable TV stations, and the crowds kept getting bigger. Some of the promoters moved the shows to bigger venues, and the band sold those out too.

The two musicians fell into a groove, with Kelly making new arrangements of all their stage material, and Kit committing them to paper. Through this collaboration, Kit also wrote out charts for 20 of Kelly's new songs. Towards the end of the tour, on May 19th, with a five-day break and two more dates left,

Kelly had to go back to California. The taping for his first performance in L.A. was set for May 25th. His first stop would be to fly to Missoula, get his camper, and make a speed run to California. He'd originally planned to stay with Michael and Terra Monapolis in Oakland and relax for a few days, but the tour with Kit was hard to leave until the last moment. Now Kelly was low on time.

"I'm sorry to say goodbye," said Kit, as he hugged Kelly at the airport ticket counter. "You made this band come alive and I thought I'd be upset by that, with you getting so much attention and all. But you lifted us up, crafted great arrangements, and made the tour more fun than it would have been without you. You paid your way in spades with the increase in ticket sales. I don't know when we'll be face to face next, so I want to say this now." Kit looked down at the floor for a long moment. He wiped his eyes.

"You're a remarkable talent, Kelly. Way better than me. Better than almost everyone out there. I hope we can make music again. I'd like to cut a CD with half your originals, and half mine. But now it's time for you to shine on your own, and me to finish the tour and kick back for a few months. Knock 'em dead on that TV show!"

They hugged again. "Kit, you're every bit the musician I am. You know that. I'm sure we'll be working together in the future. I look forward to it." With that last goodbye, Kelly checked in and boarded the plane to Montana.

In Montana Kelly got his camper out of storage, picked up another 200 CDs from Gene, and hit the road in the late afternoon. The drive through the night was a time for Kelly to assess his situation. He was going to be required to play one of his hit songs in a manner that was as close to his bestselling recording as possible. He'd been told that the network stage band had learned his tunes from his recordings with no deviations.

Kelly wasn't comfortable with this. In light of what he was producing now, his old recordings made him cringe. On the two hotel stops he made on his drive to L.A., he had been practicing his old songs and found it hard to play them in the same exact way he'd recorded them two decades ago. He had improved them, fixed issues with the lyrics, and given them all a more contemporary groove. By the time he rolled into L.A. at 9 PM on May 24th, the day before the taping of the show, he was unsure about how well he would do.

Michael and Terra were waiting for him at the hotel in L.A. "You must be exhausted from your drive!" said Terra as she hugged and kissed him.

"I'm doing okay, just a little nervous."

"Nervous?" laughed Michael. "Nervous to play those old songs? You're a shoe-in for the first cut. My niece is in touch with the producers. They already know who's going to be cut in the first show, and you're safe. A bunch of those other people have been out of the game for a while. You're tuned up."

"High strung is more accurate."

Terra changed the subject. "Let's look at the outfits I bought for you."

The trio went to the Monapolis' hotel room. Terra had spread the outfits out on the bed, the floor, and over several chairs. There were tie-dyed tee shirts, bell-bottomed pants, and lots of other silly stuff.

Kelly knew that Terra had spent long hours and lots of money on these outfits, but none of them were the old Kelly. She had never seen the Kelly Jacobs Band on stage. His stage uniform had been a blue work shirt with the sleeves rolled up, and blue jeans. He always wore cowboy boots. When the weather was cold, he went on stage with his leather flight jacket, which he had replaced and envisioned himself wearing at the first taping. He didn't know how to address all the effort Terra had gone through to compile vintage clothing.

"I want to go to my room for a quick shower," said Kelly. He'd done well to look excited about all the outfits, and now he needed a little time to formulate a response. When Kelly opened the door to his room, there were some envelopes on the floor. There was a final contract and model release, the schedule for Kelly's arrival and appearance time, and a couple of photos of Kelly from stage shots of him with his old band. Scribbled on the bottom was a note, "Look like this."

Kelly examined the photos, which were pretty blurry. In both shots he was wearing his flight jacket, jeans, and cowboy boots. He also had a moustache in both images. These photos gave Kelly an easy out for all the outfits Terra had bought, but also made him worry about having no facial hair.

"Gee, they're pretty controlling," said Terra when Kelly showed her the note and the photos.

"Yeah, they are. You've got a good pair of faded jeans, a blue work shirt, and the boots. You did great!"

Terra wasn't entirely satisfied with that, but she was glad about the jeans and the boots. The three of them had a late dinner and went directly to their rooms. Kelly was up for quite a while listening to his old recordings and figuring out the exact guitar parts. The songs sounded dated and Kelly was concerned about being seen on TV playing them so simply. It was not the way he wanted Eve to see him. He was a different person now, and if she did happen to tune in, he didn't want her to feel sorry for him participating in what he'd begun to see as a Geezerfest.

The next morning was misty and cold, which was odd for L.A. Kelly's call time at the TV studio was 2PM, so he slept late, had a big breakfast and a light lunch. Michael and Terra had tickets to be in the studio audience at the theater, which was the old movie house on the Paramount Studios lot.

Michael parked outside and wished Kelly well. Terra gave him a kiss and slipped something into his jacket. It was a small bag with a few pebbles from the island of Samos in Greece. "I keep these as good luck. You'll have to give them back when you're done with them," she said. "They're taken from a beach where Pythagoras and Epicurus walked. They'll help you. Do you have anything from Anna?"

Kelly reached inside of his shirt pocket and pulled out a lipstick tube. It was one of the few things he'd salvaged from his wrecked truck. Terra nodded in approval and gave him one last kiss.

Kelly strolled under the Paramount arch and stopped at the security office. The officer looked over Kelly's paperwork, compared him to his photograph, examined his driver's license, and told him to stand by for the shuttle. There was a lot of foot traffic on the lot. People drove by in golf carts dressed like 1800 era outlaws, Roman soldiers marched by, and showgirls pranced along practicing their dance moves. Nobody paid any attention to Kelly, or the others waiting to be picked up.

The front of the theater was covered in bright neon, glowing under dark skies. There were five camera crews roaming around and they all descended on Kelly.

"This way, Kelly," shouted several cameramen. They wanted to get a good frontal shot of Kelly and ask him a few questions. He gave each crew a little sound-bite and walked on. He was already a few minutes late.

The green room was filled with people, guitar cases, makeup artists, and even a few agents. A girl with a clipboard checked off the names of each arrival. After a performer was checked in, they were ushered over to a chair and a make up artist powdered them down. They all had old photos of each performer and some of them were trimming hair and beards to make them look like their old selves.

"You don't have a moustache," said Billy the stylist as he looked at Kelly's picture. "Didn't you get the memo? You're supposed to look like you did back in your heyday."

"This is my heyday," replied Kelly. He knew this was going to be difficult, but he had no idea it would start so soon.

"Moustache! Over here!" Billy shouted, clapping his hands.

"Is that really necessary?" asked Kelly.

"Unless you want to see me on the street, yes, it is. You don't have to wear it after today. You'll probably get cut anyway. I've never even heard of Jacob Kelly."

Kelly laughed at that. It was just the comment he needed to fortify himself. After his moustache was applied and his make up was done, Billy patted his cheek and said, "Good luck Mr. Kelly, whoever you are."

After make up and wardrobe, the contestants were herded into a ready room to hear the show director give them the rules, collect the model releases and the contracts. One man had forgotten his contract. He was asked to turn in his flowered shirt and wait to be escorted off the property.

"And then there were fifteen," said a woman next to Kelly. He turned to see her. It was Melanie Dwight, a person Kelly had shared the stage with many times. She gave him a big hug.

"Careful, Kelly, you'll lose your phony moustache!" she said, chuckling.

Kelly felt the hair on his lip and could tell it was crooked. He tore it off and threw it on the floor.

"I haven't had a moustache in 20 years. It looked stupid! This is such a cattle call, isn't it? I hope they have oxygen and popsicles for us. I feel faint already," said Kelly, a little too loudly. Most everyone laughed.

"I saw you on the news," said Melanie. "They said you'd disappeared and were found living on the street in Seattle. You'd been hit by a drunk driver and someone recognized you when you were checked into the hospital. Are you okay?"

"Really, that's what they said?" Kelly smiled. "I got broadsided by a car that ran a stop sign. When the local TV affiliate found out who I was, they concocted a wild story about me. I'm not living on the street. I have a chateau in Monaco and a house in Malibu. I was just starting a tour with Kit Wells, and the accident made me miss a few dates. But the TV coverage was good for me. The station raised some money and a local car dealer gave me a slightly used camper van. I'm gonna have more accidents. They pay better than music!"

Melanie laughed. "You look good, Kelly. And you're still a smart ass. I liked the Monaco thing. I may even stay there with you some time."

"You're the one who looks good, Melanie."

"They dyed my hair! Can you believe it? They did it with spray bottles. It only took five minutes. I'll look like a hag after I rinse it out tonight, but I feel great now!"

"Well, get used to the color because it's all gonna come down to just you and me," said Kelly.

Melanie was the first performer called out. She stood at the mic in the spotlight. Normally she played piano and sang, but her big tunes were with an orchestra. Kelly went up onto his toes to see more of the stage.

Damn, he said to himself, *they have strings down there!*

The conductor gave Melanie her note, because she started this tune a cappella. The electric performers on the side of the stage played the tune 100% accurately and Melanie nailed it. Her voice was as good as Kelly remembered it. The live audience gave her a strong applause. She was the one to beat,

125

thought Kelly. She was directed off stage-right where a camera crew was waiting to interview her.

Next up was a hard rocker with glittering tights. He was still slim and when he plugged his guitar in, he went right into a shredding solo. Kelly vaguely remembered the band. It was Kiss or Smooch, or something like that. The guy was brilliant. Several other performers followed and they were all great. Flawless in fact.

"Hey, you're Kelly Jacobs, right?" said a tall guy in a silly hippy outfit.

"Yeah, that's me."

"I thought it was you. You didn't show up at the rehearsals."

"The rehearsals?" asked Kelly.

"Yeah, there were three rehearsals. They were at a club downtown. Some people were cut back then."

"I didn't know there were rehearsals. How'd you find out about those?" asked Kelly.

"My manager."

Just then the announcer called Kelly Jacobs, and the audience gave him a loud welcome. A stage guy set up the guitar and voice microphones for Kelly. The conductor looked over his shoulder and the electric band to the side waited for Kelly's intro. His song was "Carry Me Away."

Kelly started the tune with the signature strumming, which he'd practiced. Despite his efforts to get it like his recording, his right hand persisted on giving it a deeper grove. He developed that a little bit and came in four measures later

126

than the record. The electric band made the adjustment without missing a beat, and the strings came in on the refrain. This made Kelly smile. He looked down at the conductor and winked. The crowd applauded. Kelly had never played the tune with strings because they'd been added later by the record company. The sound of a full orchestra lifted Kelly's confidence and he backed off the mic a little to let his voice open up. In just a few moments the song was over and he was waiving to the audience and walking off.

"How do you think you did?" asked the interviewer, holding up the mic for Kelly to answer.

Someone backstage interjected, "He killed it! Do you even have to ask?" This irritated the interviewer, who turned and gave the heckler a dirty look.

"Let's take this again," said the interviewer. "How do you think you did?" he asked.

Kelly gave him a big smile. "It felt good! I loved that we have a full orchestra. It was fun. I feel good about it!"

"We've heard a lot about you lately on the news. You've had some rough times. Are you hoping this is going to help re-launch your career?"

Kelly had been warned by Michael and Terra that the interviewers were going to stir things up to make it more interesting for the TV audience. It was time to give them what they wanted.

"I've had a lot of hard times, it's true. Starving times. Living in a camper for eight years and going from one low paying gig to another isn't easy. But music is my life and it's all I want to do. Sure, I could work as a leading man, a state senator, or an astronaut, but I've turned all those gigs down to play for $120 a night in roadside taverns."

The interviewer was taken aback. "You're joking, right?" he asked Kelly.

"Only about the astronaut thing. The part about playing music is true. It's all I'm designed to do and I'm gonna keep it up."

"Thanks, Kelly. Good luck to you." said the interviewer. He motioned for Kelly to go down the hallway as he readied himself for the next performer.

All of the performers sat in chairs in the large changing room. There were bottles of water, bowls of chips, and a big monitor on the wall that displayed the live stage feed. The last performer was Jeremy Patton, a top-notch pop star that still made a good living doing state fairs and festivals. Of course, he nailed it.

"This isn't going to be a cakewalk," said Kelly to Melanie. They were seated next to each other. Melanie reached over and squeezed Kelly's hand.

"No, it's not. You missed the rehearsals. There were over 40 people there. Some real sad cases. Gary Matrix was there. Remember him? 'Bad Blood' and three other number one hits. They cut him after the second rehearsal. He was a bit high and they did a breath test. The guy had smoked a joint before he went on and they canned him for it. He was really good too."

"Yeah, I remember him. He jumped off a stage once and broke a guy's shoulder," said Kelly.

"Yeah, I remember that!" Melanie laughed.

A woman in a business suit stepped onto a raised platform. The cameras were rolling behind her, getting the reactions of the performers. "When I call your name, please go over to the area behind the gold rope. Kelly Jacobs, Mark Whittier, Melanie Dwight…" She called one more name. The four performers stood next to each other. The air seemed electric with nerves. Why were there only four people set aside?

"You musicians have been selected," big pause, "to continue next week." She called up the next four. One of them was cut. This went on until only 12 remained.

Each performer was given an envelope as they exited the theater through the side stage door. Kelly and Melanie opened theirs together. There was a schedule for next week, the songs they would perform, some comments about their outfits, a voucher for a hotel in Hollywood, and a check for $1500.

"That's it? $1500? How are we supposed to live on that?" asked Kelly, smiling. "I have properties to pay for!"

"Yeah, the mortgage on your Malibu place is $1500 a day. Can I sleep there tonight?"

Kelly laughed. "I'm sorry Mel, but I'm having the gold leaf redone. I'm at the same hotel as you. But I'll buy you a drink."

"Kelly, did you even read your contract? We get meals and bar vouchers." said Melanie.

"No, of course I didn't read the contract. My legal staff takes care of that!" replied Kelly. "You can have one of my bar vouchers."

Melanie shook her head and smiled. "Next week it's another $1500 if you get cut and $3000 if you make the cut. It keeps on going up to the final four, which is $10,000 if you lose and $20,000 if you win."

"What does the winner of the final two get, besides a recording contract, which I can live without, seeing as though I'm so well known."

"The winner gets $100,000," said Melanie. "And I'm gonna love cashing that one!" She gave Kelly a pat on his butt, winked, and walked away.

Two episodes later, she was cut. Kelly was more upset than Melanie. The show went forward, and Kelly played his part as the down and out musician hoping to make a comeback. He didn't have to try very hard. He was the audience favorite. Michael and Terra came down for every show and the three of them went out for dinner after each taping.

Chapter Eighteen

When the trio sat down after the fifth taping, Michael looked serious, which was out of character because Kelly had made the cut.

"They're going to cancel the show," said Michael. "My niece told me they're looking for a replacement show. She thinks the next episode will be the last."

"But there are six competitors left. Who's gonna win?"

"I asked her that. She said they won't have a winner. Read your contract. If the show doesn't run the full season, all bets are off. They don't have to pay anyone the grand prize or fulfill their promise of a recording contract."

"I don't know what to say," replied Kelly.

"I don't either. It was a great show, and you were brilliant."

"I guess I should have gotten a clue when they had a string quartet instead of a full orchestra for the last episode. No makeup people either. They were cutting corners. The green room didn't even have bottled water."

"Yeah, when the bottom drops out, it happens quick," said Michael. "Come up and stay a while with us. I'll try my new recipes on you. I've found a few possible locations for the new Greek restaurant."

"I thought you were just going to open a souvlaki place."

Michael laughed. "Yeah, that was the plan, but it's changed. We're doing a full-blown taverna. I found a bouzouki player and everything. It's going to be great!"

"Mikey, you're an inspiration! I'll be a waiter!"

"No, you won't. We can't afford the broken dishes. But you'll play in the bar. I'm offering a free dinner and all you can earn in tips."

"Count me in. I'll see you after the last episode gets taped."

A long silence followed. Terra reached across the table and took Kelly's hand.

"I'm going to tell you a story. It's from a woman philosopher in ancient Greece. Her name was Sappho. Socrates was an admirer of hers and he told this story at a dinner party. Plato wrote it down and it appears in his famous dialog entitled the 'Symposium.' Every Greek knows it." Terra took a sip from her wine, closed her eyes, and began the story.

131

"It has been said that all of us have memories of a time before we were born. There must be some truth to this because we know how to do things that no one taught us in this lifetime. We know how to breathe. We know how to laugh. We know how to love. Loving is something we return to because we've been there before.

"Why do we join in love? There is lust, of course. But there is also the seeking of beauty. The joy of admiration. The sweet taste of nectar on the lips of your lover. And there is more.

"Man and woman were once one being. A hermaphrodite that could satisfy its own needs and never look upon another in longing. That was too perfect of a union, and the gods abhor perfection, so they split the being into a man and a woman. It was hard to do, even for the gods, and they needed axes and fire and great sharp stones. It took centuries to accomplish the complete task, because every evening when the gods rested, the being would reconstitute itself and achieve happiness. In the morning, the gods would arise from their peaceful slumber and once again be dismayed by the happiness they saw, so they would start their work again.

"Finally, the hermaphrodite was fully split and each part wept great tears that formed rushing rivers and loud waterfalls. The man part and the woman part embraced each other and tried to become one again. Their tears stopped and they joined as they once had, creating thunder and lightening and earthquakes. The joining was wonderfully pleasurable, but not permanent. They spent themselves and separated. In time, they tried to join again, with the same result of ecstasy and separation.

"All of us are the product of this unending desire to become one being again. We are made to join. One day, despite the will of the gods, two people will manage to fuse again and all of the folly that comes from this unstoppable magnetism will cease. Love will die. Until that happens, we have no control over what draws us to one another."

"That's a beautiful story," said Kelly.

Michael kissed Terra on the cheek and hugged her, then he turned to Kelly.

"You've come a long ways. The termination of this show isn't the end of your journey. You have momentum. Keep going."

"I will. Thank you two for being the best friends anyone could ever have."

The trio stood up, hugged, and said goodbye.

Kelly lay on his bed staring at the blank ceiling. He considered how he needed to follow the magnetism caused by the gods who had split man from his female counterpart. Kelly could never be happy until he found a partner that felt the same magnetism he did. Eve was that partner.

He'd had his heart set on winning the competition and it seemed as though he had more than a 50-50 chance. Now he had only one opportunity to sing Eve's birdsong on national TV. The packet he had received from the TV station gave him the song title he was expected to sing, but he wouldn't do that old tune. *What would he perform?* He hadn't written Eve's song yet. It was Sunday night. Time was getting short. The next morning he made a call.

"Hi Kit, this is Kelly. How are you doing?"

"Great! I've been watching the show. You have a good chance to win. You look like the favorite."

"That's what I'm calling you about. You can't tell anyone, but the show has been cancelled. Next Saturday night is the last episode. I need to ask a favor."

"Anything for you, Kelly."

"I'm gonna do an original tune for the last episode. It's off the script, so they may not even show it on TV. Who knows? But I want to send out this song in the hopes that the woman I met in Monterey will hear it and contact me. Can you write a string quartet arrangement for it?"

"Yeah, I can try. Can you send me a chart and a recording?"

"I haven't written it yet," said Kelly.

There was a long pause. "I'm sorry, you're breaking up. It sounded like you said you haven't written it yet."

"Yeah, that's right. I need to compose the song. I can get it done by Wednesday. Can you put together a string quartet arrangement on Thursday and Friday and get it to me Friday night?"

"Kelly, you're asking me to move mountains. I haven't written for a string quartet since college. I'm not the right guy for this."

"You're the perfect guy for this. It's a lot to ask, I know. You've done a lot for me this last year."

"Kelly, you're the one that's come through for me. I got a contract to take the band on a European tour. The CD is selling like mad. I owe you, man."

"Can you do the arrangement?"

"Yes, I can. Just get it to me before midnight on Wednesday. I owe you big time," said Kit. "Now I've got a favor to ask of you."

"Anything. Whatever you need," replied Kelly.

"Can you come to Europe with me? It's a five-month tour. It will give us a lot of time to work on our material and release a duo album."

"Done," replied Kelly.

"Okay. Get me a rough chart and a recording by Wednesday night. I'll look for it by email."

"Thanks, Kit!"

They hung up. Kit was already lamenting his response and Kelly was wondering how he'd get the song written in the next two days. As soon as he set the phone down, he picked up his guitar and started to play some familiar patterns. It was no use. It wasn't a guitar tune he wanted, it was a piano ballad.

The next morning Kelly looked up piano dealers. The biggest one was only a few blocks from his hotel. He walked in, sat down at a grand piano, and started playing a Bach two-part invention. The salesman approached him and stood by patiently. When Kelly finished, the salesman asked, "Are you interested in a concert grand, or a studio grand?"

Kelly had chosen the most expensive piano in the store and the salesman identified Kelly as a qualified buyer by his command of the keys.

"I'm just starting my search. It will be a while before I'm ready to buy."

"Hey, you're the guy on the TV show. Jacobs, right? Kelly Jacobs. I watch the show all the time. You're gonna win. I'm sure of it! I didn't know you could play piano. You're a trained classical player. That's obvious."

"Thanks for your vote of confidence. I hope to win. I'm going to play piano on the next episode. I need to complete the composition. Is there a quiet practice room I can use to work on it?"

"Sure. We have two rooms at the end of hall. There's an upright in one room and a baby grand in the other."

"One other thing," said Kelly. "They don't have a piano on stage. If I let you guys put a sign on a piano, could you have one delivered to Paramount Studios for the next taping?"

"Ah, I don't know. That's a question for the owner. He'll be back in a few hours."

"Okay, I'll be in the baby grand room. Please let me know what he decides."

Kelly sat at the baby grand and put his yellow writing pad and pencil on the music stand. For the first time in his life, he was stymied. He just sat there and thought about what he wanted to say to Eve. It took almost an hour before the ideas started flowing.

136

The composition was entitled "Until Monterey." It was a torch song, which Kelly had never written before. There was nothing familiar about any of it. The chord changes were foreign, there was no insistent groove, and the melody was intricate, unlike the hooks that Kelly usually employed. Once he got it going, it just flowed out of his fingers. By the time the owner of the piano store entered the room, Kelly was finished with the song.

"That's a nice song. I've never heard it", said Greg Donner, a short man in a suit. "I've been following the show on TV. Edward said you'd like to have a piano delivered to the Paramount lot in exchange for promotional consideration. That sounds good to me. When would you like it delivered? We already have a sign to hang on the end of the piano. We've done this before."

Kelly stood up and shook Mr. Donner's hand. "The piano needs to be in place for the taping at 2 PM on Saturday. As you know, the show is live, so as soon as it's finished you can load up the piano and take it away. I'll arrange for your truck to be cleared at the gate. Thank you for your help on this. The piano in the theater is really bad!"

"No need to thank us. We always appreciate a chance to get a plug in for our shop. So what's the story behind that song? Are you going to perform it on the show?"

"That's the plan. I need a video of it to use as reference for a string arrangement I'm working on. I think my phone does video. Would you mind doing the honors?" Kelly handed his phone to Mr. Donner, who said he knew how to operate it.

"Any time you're ready," said Mr. Donner. Kelly gave him the sign, counted to four, and played the song from start to finish in two minutes and fifty seconds. It was just shy of the three-minute maximum set by the show's producers.

Kelly took his phone back and with Mr. Donner's help, replayed the video to make sure it was okay.

"Thank you, Mr. Donner. I'll see your guys at the Paramount theater at 1 PM." They shook hands again and Kelly left the store with a video, his song notes, and a promise to have a piano on stage for the final taping of the show. Kelly had no idea how he'd manage to get the piano through front gate security. Everything was a long shot, but the rule set by Anna was to succeed or die trying.

Chapter Nineteen

Kelly managed to send the video of the song and a picture of his handwritten chart to Kit around midday on Wednesday, 11 hours ahead of schedule. There were some tweaks Kelly would have wanted to make to the song, but it was very good as is. There was something that Kelly liked about first takes. They were honest and soulful. Too much rehearsal hurt the feeling of a performance. Kelly had operated with this brand of brinksmanship in his band days, distributing rough charts to the band right on stage during a performance. The band and the audience loved it. They felt like they were a part of the creative process. He hadn't done anything like this until his time on the road with Kit Wells. It felt great.

Kelly's next challenge was to figure out how to get the baby grand piano past the front gate and delivered to the stage of the Paramount theater. The whole plan would fail if that step wasn't accomplished. Another phone call was needed.

"Hey Jack, this is Kelly. How are you?"

Jack was drying glasses and hanging them up above the bar at the Bluebird Café in Monterey. "Hey Irish, we've been watching you on TV. You're gonna win. I'm betting on it!"

"Please tell me you're not betting on the outcome."

"Just a little bet," said Jack.

"See if you can withdraw it."

"Why? Do you have a fix?"

"No, nothing like that. They're planning to cancel the show and there won't be a winner."

"Oh. That's not good," said Jack. "But you're not calling me about that, are you? You need a favor."

"Yes, Jack, I do. Was Carl successful in finding out where Eve moved? Did he get an address for her?"

"No. He sent a letter to the house she lived in and it was returned. Unfortunately, the house was sold and the new owners don't have her forwarding address. It makes it impossible to contact her, unless you get her to hear the song. Did you write the song?"

"Yes, I did. It's the best thing I've ever done and if she hears it, she'll know it's for her. I'm sure of it."

"So how are you going to have her hear it if the show is going to be cancelled?"

Kelly had thought about how to present this next part of the conversation, but he hadn't managed to work it out, so he just asked the favor right up front. "There's going to be one more episode. But there's a hurdle I have to get over. Jack, can Carl get a piano delivery onto the security man's clipboard at the gates of Paramount Studios?"

"Rewind, Irish. You want Carl, who you've only met once, to arrange for the security man to let a piano delivery through the front gate at Paramount Studios in Hollywood, California. Do I have that right?"

"Exactly. The piano will come in a van from Donner Piano Company at 1 PM this Saturday. The piano guys will roll it onto the stage in time for the 2 PM taping, and take it away after the show."

"Is there anything else?" asked Jack.

"So Carl can do that?"

"Of course not! Are you out of your mind? How would Carl be able to get the okay for a piano delivery into Paramount Studios?"

"He's good with computers. I saw the website he put together showing me in Moscow. Isn't it possible that he can do this by computer? I don't know how this stuff works."

"Yeah, that's painfully obvious, Irish. If you want a piano, why don't you ask for one? I'm sure they have one on stage."

"Yes, they do, but the back up band is using it. Besides, the producers tell us what song to play. They won't let me play a song on piano. Kelly Jacobs didn't play piano. My only chance is to have one delivered so it's on stage when I get my call."

"It's bold, I'll give you that. I don't see how this is going to be possible, but I'll work on it."

"Thanks, Jack. I'll check in with you on Friday."

Kelly kicked off his boots and laid down on his bed. It felt good to stretch out. He'd gotten a lot accomplished today. Of course there were loose ends, *but things would either work out, or they wouldn't.*

By Friday morning Kelly was feeling pretty good about the Saturday taping. He called Jack to see if Carl had made any progress. Jack's messages were going into voice mail. Kelly tried several more times, but eventually gave up. It was obvious that Jack wasn't answering his phone. Kelly called the Bluebird, but the girl answering the phone said that Jack was too busy to take a call. Kelly left a message.

By Saturday at 10 AM, Kelly hadn't heard from Jack, so he finished his breakfast and started rehearsing the song on the guitar. It wasn't a guitar song, and the charts that Kit had written started with a piano intro. If Kelly was forced to play the tune solo on his guitar he wasn't sure it would be effective. It wasn't a good fallback position. Kelly got dressed and set out for the studio. He wanted to get there early and see what he could do to make things right.

At the gate he said hello to the guard, who motioned him through. Kelly was a familiar face by now. He stood by the shuttle stop for a few minutes and then walked back to the guard.

"Did you get a notification about a piano delivery to the theater?"

The guard looked at his clipboard, flipped some pages, and shook his head. "Nothing yet. They're bad about that kind of thing. Where's it coming from?"

"Donner Piano Company. Should be here at the gate no later than one o'clock. Taping starts at two."

"I'll be looking for it," said the guard, flipping through the pages again.

Just as Kelly was turning away, a bicycle messenger entered the gate, slipping in behind the security guard, circling around and pulling to stop in front of him. To the guard, it looked as if the messenger had pedaled from inside the complex. He handed the guard a form.

"Here it is," said the guard to Kelly. "Expect a delivery from Donner Piano. Okay, we're set." The guard dropped the clipboard to his side and approached a limo that had just driven up. The messenger looked up at Kelly and winked. It was Jack's boyfriend Carl. He turned his bike around and rode off.

Chapter Twenty

Kelly decided to walk to the studio instead of taking the shuttle. Paramount Studios is big, but over the last few weeks he'd become familiar with the route. Kelly was passed by the Donner Piano delivery van on his way. There was still a big chance that it would be turned away at the theater, but there was nothing he could do now, other than hope Anna had it worked out.

A golf cart passed by carrying some young girls in bathing suits. They shouted, "Good luck, Kelly!"

At the theater loading door Kelly could see the delivery guys being held up by security. One of the assistant producers of the show was looking through his papers to check on the need for a piano. He was agitated. When the assistant saw Kelly, he motioned for him to come over.

"You ordered a baby grand to be delivered on stage for today's taping? Who okayed that?" he demanded. He wasn't a day over 21.

"Matthew. I told him I needed it for my song today."

"Matthew isn't with us anymore. He's moved on. He hasn't been here for two weeks."

Kelly knew that. "Well how am I gonna play my song without a piano?"

"You're a guitar player! You don't play piano on this show! You play the guitar and sing your out-of-date songs and hope you don't get cut! That's what you do!" The kid was fuming.

Kelly stood his ground. If this kid was the only thing standing in the way of him singing his song to Eve, he either had to go around him or through him.

"I'm not a guitar player. I'm the son-in-law of George Jacobs, the guy that signs your check, punk! Now get out of the way so we can get my piano on stage!"

The kid became confused. He turned to the delivery guys. "Okay, put the damn thing on the stage and get it off the minute Mr. Kelly 'has been' Jacobs is done. You guys got it?"

They nodded. Kelly nodded. The assistant producer kid didn't nod. "You're on first, now that this thing has screwed up my schedule!"

"Okay," Kelly said, walking past him.

Once inside the theater, he applied powder to his face, drank some water directly from the tap by leaning over the sink, and consulted the clock. It was twenty minutes till show time.

The musicians were tuning up. There was still a string quartet, which he was thankful for.

Kelly removed his jacket and jeans to reveal a more modern outfit. He waited in the wings, fidgeting with his guitar. The piano was in place and the lighting grips on the upper gantry were moving some spots to accommodate the change.

One of the guys from Donner piano asked Kelly, "Who is George Jacobs?"

"I have no idea!" Kelly replied. The guys from Donner piano laughed.

As the clock ticked down and the theater filled up, Kelly arranged his charts for quick distribution. The red tally light flashed at the back of the theater signaling that cameras were rolling. The show would be live in five minutes.

Kelly walked to the end of the stage and handed the string charts to the conductor. The man had a confused look on his face that quickly turned to irritation. Kelly didn't stay to see what happened next. Then he went over to the stage band and

144

distributed their charts. The players there were also puzzled, but Kelly walked away before they could raise an objection.

The house manager came onto the control mic. "Ten seconds to live broadcast. Nine, eight, seven, six, five…"

Bob Nevin, the pompous ass fronting the show, stepped on his marks and the spotlight hit him. "Welcome ladies and gentlemen! We have six contestants today. I'm told that the first one will be Kelly Jacobs. This time he's playing piano. The title of his song has been crossed out on my cue card, so I have no idea what he's going to play! Let's hear it for Kelly Jacobs!"

A loud applause followed.

The stage lights went dark and a blue shaft of light hit Kelly from behind as he walked onto the stage and sat at the piano bench. His body was outlined by the spotlight, making him look like he was wearing form fitting neon. It left his face in darkness.

He could see the string section in the pit studying the charts. Kelly had never heard the arrangement, so he wouldn't know if it was being played correctly or not. The whole thing was a crapshoot that started with a piano intro.

Kelly had never played a piano intro for this song. In fact, he'd only played the song in the piano store a few times. He placed his fingers on the ivory keys and slid them back and forth to find the tipping point. There was the feeling of a gentle hand on his shoulder, and he knew not to look over to see who it was. A yellow spotlight was focused on Kelly's face and it grew brighter as he began the piano intro Kit had written for him. It was good. The strings came in and then the drums and bass took up the slow tempo. He closed his eyes and began to sing.

145

Kelly's voice was loud and rich. He had to back away from the mic so he could let loose and not overpower the tune. The strings swelled in volume and the electric band locked with his piano parts. Kelly was riding a wave. The lyrics poured from his heart without effort. He didn't know if they were the ones he'd recorded on the video he'd sent to Kit or not. The important thing was his call to Eve. Every word and phrase was a way to ask her to come to him. He sang the last line three times and let the final chord ring. The house was absolutely silent until one person started clapping. Then there was an uproar. He got up from the bench and bowed deeply. The applause increased. It was over. He'd done what he needed to do. Anna had helped. He could feel her hand squeeze his shoulder one more time and fade away. She was gone now. The audience kept cheering and Kelly bowed again and walked off stage.

The interviewer was waiting with his mic. Cameras were rolling. Questions were asked. Kelly had no recollection of any of that. He took his packet from the producer's desk as he left the theater and opened it up when he was outside. There was a note and his check.

We are sorry to announce that the show has been dropped. This is your final payment for services. According to the conditions of the contract, we have fulfilled our obligations. Thank you for your services and good luck.

Michael and Terra were at the gate waiting for him. They joined together for dinner as usual. It was a subdued affair and Michael and Terra left early to catch a flight back to Oakland.

That night at nine o'clock in his hotel room, Kelly tuned into NBC to watch the last episode of "Where Are They Now?"

The show began as usual, but the first act was not Kelly, it was Carly Warren, a country singer. Kelly watched each performer, and as the clock ticked down, he wasn't among them. There was an unusually long commercial break, and the show came back on. There was Bob Nevin introducing Kelly. They edited out his comments and cut right to Kelly at the piano.

Chapter Twenty-One

Eve and Maria watched the show every week, and were disappointed that Kelly didn't come on this time. There were only minutes before it was over. Eve dragged herself up from the couch and headed for her bedroom.

"Come back, he's on now!" yelled Maria to Eve.

"Oh my god, they didn't cut him!" said Eve. She ran into the room and dropped back onto the couch.

"He plays piano?" asked Maria.

"Shhhh!"

A lone spotlight hit Kelly. It was a deep blue. His face was in dark shadow. A faint purple glow developed on his hair and shoulders. The view went to a wide shot where Kelly sat still on a black stage, radiating from his dramatic lighting. He was dressed in a dark suit coat and burgundy collarless shirt. The scene cut to a close up of his fingers moving silently on the keys. He played a single note, then two, then an undulating current of notes that rode on top of one another. The camera pulled back to reveal his face, eyes closed.

147

A Beggar's Tune

The strings came in and lifted the tune to an elegant level. Kelly raised his face and it glowed in a bright column of golden light. He began singing.

It was long, it seemed so long ago,
I asked myself, still I just don't know,
I don't have the answers, for the time of you and I,
The memories I cling to, in the corners of my mind,
There was dancing, under the moonlight,
I dreamed and I hoped, it would go on and on,
But after my last song, the music was all gone,

Until Monterey, I can still hear you say,
It's too much, Baby, I need some time away,
What I did not know, that was your way to say goodbye.

Goodbye, baby.

There were dreams, dreams of a future
You gave me in a box, all the secrets that we shared,
There were teardrops, that I shed, when we parted ways,
I'd have held you forever, I wish I'd thought to stay,

Until Monterey, can you hear me say?
I'm coming back, but need some time away,
I should have known, a kiss was your way to say goodbye
Goodbye Baby, I did not know,

That was your way to say goodbye.
Come back to me baby, I can't stand you being away.
Come back. It's all I have the strength to say,
Come back baby.

Kelly ended the song and held the last chord. There was
no applause at first, just silence, then the audience was on their
feet clapping and shouting. Kelly stood up and bowed. The
crowd noise didn't taper off. He smiled and bowed again. The
house lights began to come up and he walked off stage.

The credits rolled over a shot of the audience waving
their arms, whistling, stomping their feet, and shouting.

Eve tasted salty tears and covered her face. She couldn't
move.

"Are you okay?" asked Maria.

Eve nodded silently.

The next week Maria and Eve were on the couch, ready
for the episode, but a rerun of a crime drama came on. They
checked the TV listings, but "Where Are They Now?" couldn't
be found. Eve was frantic. Maria called the cable TV company
but only got a request to leave a message.

Maria spent the night on a chair in Eve's bedroom so
Eve wouldn't be alone. Maria got a few hours of sleep, but Eve
did not. The next evening the two women went to the Bluebird
Café and asked Jack if they knew what happened to the show.

"It was cancelled. Kelly knew it was going to happen, so
he played that song for you."

"Where is he? Do you have a number for him?" asked Eve.

"He's on the road with the Kit Wells Band. They're finishing a tour. I think their last date is in Cincinnati next week. I don't have his number. He'll be coming out here in two months. I've got him on my calendar. If he calls, what do you want me to tell him? I'm sure he wants to see you."

"Tell him Eve is waiting for him. Here's my number."

A week later Kelly called Jack and left a message that he wouldn't be coming back to Monterey for his dates at the Bluebird Café. He and Kit Wells were going on a European tour, and Kelly was going to hunker down with Kit and rehearse like mad.

"I'm sorry to cancel on you, Jack, but this opportunity with Kit is my big chance. If you should see or hear from Eve, please give her my number." Kelly spoke slowly and clearly, making sure there could be no mistakes in the number, then he said goodbye, and hung up.

Jack called Eve with the information. She didn't act on it right away.

Kelly is famous again and touring. He won't have time to see me. He's probably all the way on the other side of the country.

Maria urged her to call, and Eve said she would, but she was afraid of being rejected. It would be bad, almost like losing Will. Kelly had helped her, but he hadn't made an effort to find her. Writing a song about their time together was a beautiful gesture, but Eve didn't believe it meant that Kelly wanted her. She kept putting off calling him to protect herself.

Chapter Twenty-Two

Three months after the final airing of the TV episode, and long after the show had slipped out of the memory of the public, all the members of the Kit and Kelly Band were preparing for their trip. Kelly gave Jack one more call to see if he'd had any contact with Eve but all he got was Jack's voice mail.

"Hey Jack, I'm leaving with Kit Wells for London tonight from San Francisco. I want to thank you for your help and support. All the best."

An hour later Jack played his messages. He sat in a chair, thinking about what to do.

Eve's cell phone rang. "Hello?"

"Eve, this is Jack from the Bluebird Café. Did you and Kelly ever connect?"

"No, I never called him."

"Eve, this is none of my business, but, well, it is my business. I like you both and you belong together. Get in the car and go to him. He's leaving for London from San Francisco in a few hours. Go. Go right now!"

Eve began her long drive to San Francisco. The traffic was awful and she tried to calm herself by listening the radio, but Kelly's song kept playing in her mind.

Four hours later the band was at the San Francisco airport, waiting in line at the British Airways desk to get their boarding passes. It was the first stop on a 21-city tour. The band would be gone from December through July, returning on the 4th.

Kelly hadn't heard from Eve, and had given up hoping he would. Every time he began to dial her number on his phone, he stopped and hung up. What did he have to offer her? She wouldn't leave her comfortable life for a traveling musician. His career was picking up, and that meant more travel. He knew that leaving the U.S. meant any chance of finding her would drop to zero.

Yes, there were the romantic Greek myths, but they were only stories.

"Where's Becky?" asked Kit. Everyone was accounted for except her. This wasn't the first time she'd been late, but it was likely to be the last. She was a good road manager, but not always sober.

"I saw her going into the bathroom over there," said Kato, pointing to a restroom sign. "She was looking bad. Sorry to say it, but she'd been drinking. She broke up with her man and it knocked her off the wagon. It's not good, Kit."

As the band was discussing what to do, a woman ran across the terminal floor toward the group.

"Jacob! It's me!" She was waving.

Kelly turned and spread his arms. Eve flew into his embrace. They held onto each other and kissed.

"I wanted to see you, but I couldn't get up the courage. Then Jack called and told me you were leaving for England tonight. I couldn't help myself. I wanted to see you!"

152

Kelly kept kissing her.

"Hi, my name is Kit. You must be the woman Kelly has been talking about every waking moment. I thought he was exaggerating, but I can see he wasn't." He extended a hand to her. "I'm sorry to break this up, but we have to get to the terminal. We board in 35 minutes."

"I can take the next flight," Kelly suggested. Kit shook his head.

Kit turned to Eve. "What are you doing tonight?"

"Just saying goodbye to Jacob and driving back to Monterey. Why?"

Kit turned on his heel and walked toward the ladies restroom. He pushed through the door and went inside. In a couple of minutes he came out with something in his hand.

"If you've got nothing else planned, you're with us. You're now a road manager in training. Your name is Becky Eliott. Here's your passport and California I.D. Step up and get your ticket. We don't want to miss this flight."

"But my car is in the passenger loading zone!"

"Is that it?" Kato said, pointing to a silver Toyota being towed away.

"Yes," replied Eve.

"Get your ticket, Becky Eliott, so we can start this adventure," said Kit.

Kelly looked at her. "Please come with me, Eve. We won't get another chance. This is it."

Eve kissed him, and went to the desk, stepping in front of a line of people. She handed the passport to the ground hostess, who opened it up and saw a driver's license inside. She checked the numbers, looked at Eve, and issued the tickets. They all ran to the terminal, getting there just in time.

Eve and Kelly found their seats in first class. They held hands as the crew readied for takeoff.

"You heard the song, didn't you?" Kelly asked.

"Of course, I did. I only heard it once, but it kept playing in my mind, over and over. Even in my dreams."

"Why didn't you call me after you heard it?"

"For the same reason you didn't call me. We're frightened," Eve said, looking out the window. She turned to Kelly. "Don't leave me Jacob. Please don't. I won't survive it again."

"I promise I won't if you won't," replied Kelly. "What made you change your mind and come to the airport?"

"Jack called me a few hours ago and told me to drop everything and go to you. He said it was our last chance. I would have called you eventually, but knowing you were leaving made things urgent. When they award the Grammy for 'Until Monterey', it should go to Jacob and Jack."

Kelly brought Eve close and they kissed.

The jetliner taxied into position, gathered speed and lifted up into the cold San Francisco night. Jacob and Eve were headed for London and points beyond.

The End.

Made in the USA
Columbia, SC
29 July 2022

64277331R00085